# THE DEATH OF THE WIZARD MERLIN

by

## BARAK A. BASSMAN

TELEMACHUS PRESS

**THE DEATH OF THE WIZARD MERLIN**


Cover designed by Telemachus Press, LLC

Cover art:
Copyright © iStock_612234690_duncan1890

Published by Telemachus Press, LLC
7652 Sawmill Road
Suite 304
Dublin, Ohio 43016
http://www.telemachuspress.com

ISBN: 978-1-951744-04-5 (eBook)
ISBN: 978-1-951744-05-2 (Paperback)

Library of Congress Control Number: 2020900118

**FICTION**/Fantasy/Arthurian

Version 2020.01.06

# Table of Contents


I. A Wizard Adrift — 1

II. The Wizard's Longing — 5

III. The Nun's Rebuke — 19

IV. How the Wizard Fell from Grace — 26

V. How Merlin Counseled King Uther Pendragon — 43

VI. The True Importance of Magic — 64

VII. A Happy Idyll — 70

VIII. The Snake in the Garden — 75

IX. The Wages of Sin — 85

Other Books by Barak Bassman — 91

# THE DEATH OF THE WIZARD MERLIN

# I. A Wizard Adrift

ALTHOUGH THE KNIGHTS jousting on the meadow were in high spirits under the clear summer sky, Merlin the Enchanter, who was far too short and too fat to ride a horse well (and whose tangled beard would always catch in the reins), was not sure what to do with himself. Earlier in the day, he had been sitting next to King Arthur, reminiscing about battles from long ago when Arthur had subdued the Saxon warlords. Yet, after a few minutes, King Arthur, prodded by Queen Guinevere and the other lovely ladies of the court, had turned away from Merlin to focus instead on the dashing and graceful knights sparring on the field.

But armed men on horseback knocking each other to the ground did not interest Merlin. Just imagine, he mused, if one of these knights were to be so enchanted that he thought himself to be a field mouse—or that his opponents were giant owls—or maybe that he was bleeding profusely from a phantom wound in his belly. The bewitched knight would wail in terror like a frightened child and scatter to the winds. The image made him smile.

After his brief conversation with Arthur, he had shuffled down from the stands where the King and Queen were sitting and wandered barefoot about the edges of the wide meadow. Wherever he went, the spectators made a wide berth to let him pass. Eventually he squatted down alone on a flat rock and picked at the furry moss. He mumbled some words in an obscure language and a white rose sprouted up. He mumbled something else and it withered away. Then he did the same with a red rose and a yellow rose and a pink rose. After a while this too bored him.

Merlin looked up at the crowds watching the knights fight each other. There was wild cheering, and faces twitched in anticipation for what would happen next. He wondered why he had spent so much of his life toiling away for these people who, now that they could at last enjoy a respite of peace and prosperity, wanted nothing more than to watch men knock each other off horses and beat each other with swords. And for what? To be applauded by strangers and awarded a garland of flowers from the Queen? Half these fool knights, if not more, would get themselves seriously hurt at these games, rendering them incapable of defending Logres should a real enemy care to attack King Arthur's realm. And of course once Arthur realized that he had yet again stupidly permitted so many of his vital heavy cavalry troops to be wounded in this silly tournament, he would beg his ever faithful Merlin to mix the herbs and ointments and potions that would heal them.

Seeking a distraction from his troubled thoughts, his eyes wandered about the meadow, until they found their way to her—tall and willowy, with thick red hair falling far down her back, her loose blue gown tussled slightly by the wind. He stared intensely at her, stared and daydreamed, losing track of everything around him except for the easy, lazy swaying motions of her body.

But then she turned her head and met his stare. Covering her face with her hands, she ducked behind another woman, a nun with a wrinkled face who scowled angrily backed at him. The nun crossed herself several times and seemed to be praying to her god. The Christian priests were not fond of Merlin.

A knight in white armor, streaked with dirt and blood, rushed over to the distraught girl. Her lover? Her brother? He was not sure. The knight unstrapped his helmet and bent down to speak to her. When the knight stood up again he started walking towards Merlin with his sword drawn. Merlin wondered what this angry young knight thought he was going to do.

Before the knight had gone far, Sir Gawain intercepted him and threw him to the ground. You idiot, Gawain said, do you think your weapons will be any use against Merlin the Enchanter? He will confuse your reason or afflict you with sores and boils. And the King would not appreciate harm coming to Merlin, who will be needed to heal all these wounded knights, including you. Off with you, fool, get away from here.

Although the humbled knight harmlessly scampered off, the lovely girl had disappeared. Merlin sighed. With the girl gone from his sight, this was to be a long, dull day.

# II. The Wizard's Longing

AS MERLIN HAD feared, the tournament left dozens of young, previously healthy knights writhing and moaning with broken bones and deep puncture wounds all over their bodies. When the fighting finally ended and the elegant lords and ladies of Arthur's court retired to a joyous night of feasting and drinking with the few knights who had emerged both victorious and physically intact, Merlin organized the servants to tend to the wounded men and to transport them on straw mattresses to a nearby abbey.

In the days and weeks that followed, Merlin would travel each morning to that abbey to supervise their care. The monks would look at Merlin with disgust, crossing themselves whenever he passed in the hallways. One particularly fervent brother threw a cup of holy water into Merlin's face. And as Merlin knew would happen, the good Christian brothers refused to administer his potions and ointments and herbs, which they denounced as witchcraft and devilry.

So Merlin was compelled to go alone from one straw mattress to another to administer the proper healing remedies and spells for each wounded knight. At least the knights expressed their gratitude for his ministrations and offered him kind words.

They would also beg him for news from their homes. With sufficient concentration and the appropriate incantations, Merlin was able to see events unfolding far away in place or in time, and from these visions he could ease their worries about family members and lovers and estates. But the monks swore again—and with ever louder indignation—that these were demon's tricks, and the knights were being seduced into losing their immortal souls so that they could catch up on silly local gossip.

Once Merlin was able to depart the abbey, he would walk into the forest beyond the meadow to collect the herbs he needed for the various knights' treatments. Sometimes he spoke to the birds or the squirrels to help pass the time. Being alone in the woods soothed his nerves.

When the sun fell from the sky, Merlin would return to the castle keep. He was staying in a special room, down in the cellar, which he locked with a series of enchantments. There he mixed his ointments and potions until King Arthur's summons to the evening banquet.

With a heavy sigh, he would trudge slowly up to Arthur's great hall. By the time his flabby, stubby legs had mounted all the high steps, the banquet would have started, but the King always kept a seat next to him empty, waiting for Merlin.

The food at these banquets was not to Merlin's taste. He preferred fruits, nuts, and vegetables, picked right from the tree or bush. But Arthur's cook knew nothing of fruits and nuts and little of vegetables either. The lords and ladies of Logres seemed to eat nothing but fatty chunks of venison and pork floating in viscous cream sauces, which they washed down with bitter ale.

In between raising toasts and swapping stories about hunting boars, King Arthur would bend down and whisper feverishly with Merlin. Had Merlin seen a vision about this or that lord around the table—was he loyal? Were his liegemen happy? Did he pay his smiths well to arm and equip his knights? What about enemies abroad—Saxons, Irish, Cornish—were they on the move? Plotting, conspiring? And Merlin would advise the King as best he could, although he was always reminding His Grace that his visions were often brief and unclear.

It was at the King's banquet on the third night after the tournament, after he had finally convinced King Arthur that the Irish had no intention of raiding his lands, that Merlin, feeling bored, set his eyes to wandering about the room, from the reddish drunken faces bobbing up and down to the servants hauling piles of venison chunks onto the table to the earnestly grim tapestries on the walls depicting pious Christian scenes of the Virgin and Child.

And then he saw her again: the red-headed girl from the tournament. She was in a corner, next to the same nun and another older woman, a lady of the court whose skin had wrinkled and pruned with her long years. They were speaking animatedly, although they were too far away for him to make out the conversation. The red-haired girl was wearing a tight red gown, and when she blushed, she appeared to be a pillar of glowing red twilight.

Once more, Merlin stared at her, losing all sense of the passing of time or what anyone else may have been saying or doing. He knew the girl and many others would be furious if they realized what he was doing, but he could not bear to look away from her. As he watched her, he felt both excited and soothed at the same time.

But then Merlin's name began to be shouted loudly about in the banquet hall. As he learned later, there had been a heated argument about whether King Vortigern, whom Arthur's father, Uther Pendragon, had overthrown, was a noble knight or a treacherous coward. The drunken debaters eventually recalled that Merlin had actually known Vortigern and prophesied his demise with the marvel of the red dragon and the white dragon fighting in the sky. So they naturally wanted to ask his opinion of the matter.

But he did not hear them calling his name, enraptured as he was by sight of the red-haired girl. And as the banqueters shrieked his name ever more loudly, all eyes in the great hall turned towards Merlin so that everyone could now clearly see what he had been doing. The red-haired girl screamed and covered her head in shame, and the nun and the elderly matron quickly blocked her from view and ushered her out a side door.

Merlin now felt angry eyes boring into him. Some of the knights fumbled for their weapons, presumably to defend the girl's honor, but they were too drunk to do any real harm. King Arthur gently suggested that Merlin retire for the evening, as he had a great deal of work to do in the morning tending to the sick and wounded. He bowed his head and mutely obeyed. But he did not feel safe from those heated glares until he was behind his cellar room doors again, securely locked in by his enchantments.

The next evening, when he dined again at the King's table, Merlin craned his neck for another glimpse of the red-haired girl—a quick one, he told himself, just enough to be a balm for the restless stirring inside him, but then he would turn away, yes, immediately, so no one would notice and accuse him of shaming her—but wherever he looked, he could not find her.

Perhaps she is late to the feast, he thought. Yet no matter how long he waited, she did not show. He considered casting a spell to see where she was, but he had trouble concentrating—there were so many loud arguments between the drunken knights, and Arthur kept pestering him with questions about whether this knight or that other knight was healing well in the abbey. But most of all, he had a terrible, anxious trembling in his limbs from both his longing to see the girl and his shame at himself for this pitiful yearning.

And why, Merlin's thoughts continued, should she be anything but embarrassed and disgusted by his leering? He was not handsome and tall like the knights of Arthur's Court, nor was he young. He had no lands or titles. And he did not follow Christian ways, so the nun by her side—that miserable shriveled up old woman with a face like a brittle dead leaf—must be poisoning her against him, calling him a demon's child and cursing his art as the tricks of the Devil.

Still, he could offer wealth—he could conjure as much gold or silver or jewels as the red-haired girl could ever desire. When Arthur was first crowned King and many of his barons refused to recognize his claim to the throne, Merlin had used his spells to summon heaps of gold bars to give to the wicked barons' knights to persuade them to pledge fealty to the new King. He could easily do the same for her.

Yet what would he ask in exchange for the gold? He could not ask to lay with her and take her maidenhood—she would detest him even more for trying to dishonor her as if she were a whore. He could propose marriage. He supposed he would need to be baptized, but he could do that—the move would anger certain fairies, true, but they would forgive him. And anyway, they had done nothing to fetch him a bride. That is it, he thought: He, Merlin the Enchanter, would offer the girl mountains of gold if she would marry him, and he would toss in his baptism, too, which should please the nun.

But what would he do then? He did not want to live in a castle, and she would not want to sleep in a forest. Their children would inherit no titles or lands, and if something happened to Merlin, the magic could slip away, leaving the family impoverished. Seeking a reprieve from these melancholy thoughts, Merlin looked up again, both hoping and dreading to see the red-haired girl. But she was still not there.

Two drunken knights were quarreling about which one had killed a boar on that day's hunt. Their companions egged them on, supporting one claim now, then the other, everyone guzzling dark, thick ale like ravenous bears gorging at a lake. Soon the two men came to blows, until, at King Arthur's command, Sir Kay the Seneschal separated them and had each man escorted to a different room to go to sleep for the night.

The room then quieted down. The remaining knights were drinking their last, sullen gulps before slinking away in silence to their mattresses. Now that there were no distractions, Merlin tried to cast a spell to see where the red-haired girl was. He started reciting the incantation, with steady concentration, but then reached the part where he had to name her—the spirits whom he was summoning to do his bidding needed some identifying description beyond pretty maiden with long red hair—and he realized, with a shock, that he did not know her name.

Merlin stepped down from his seat and walked down the side of the table until he reached Queen Guinevere. He asked to speak to Her Grace for a moment. She gracefully rose, took his hand, and led him into a corner. She arched her back to bend her eyes far down to his level, as she was easily a head and then some taller than him, and her thick golden hair fell forward like a canopy to shield him from the ugliness of the overturned ale jugs around the room. That hair smelled sweet and fresh—floral—and he had an impulse to grab those sweet-smelling blonde sunbeams and rub them on his cheeks. But then he remembered himself again—there were limits, real limits, in the court at Logres, even for him.

My Lord Merlin, you had some matter to discuss with me?

Yes, My Lady, Your Grace … there was a girl, a maiden … she was here last night, I saw her, but now she, well, she is not here … she had red hair … would Your Grace by chance happen to know her name? I had not made her acquaintance yet, and I was curious about a new lady at the court.

While he spoke Merlin had looked down toward the ground, to where Guinevere's long golden gown had clumped up against the floor tiles. When he looked up again, he saw Guinevere's eyes burning with hate. Merlin felt a terrible dread, as if he had committed an awful crime, although it was, he assured himself, a simple inquiry of the sort that could not be questioned—a harmless bit of curiosity about someone new at the court.

After a long pause, she answered him in a voice that was unsettlingly calm: My Lord Merlin, there are many young maidens who came for the tournament and have yet to return home. I could not possibly know which lady you mean—they are all so lovely and young and happy. Do not concern yourself with them. I will look after the maidens of Logres and ensure they find good Christian husbands and birth good Christian knights. I know you are greatly burdened caring for the sick and the wounded at the abbey, and you do not want to add more troubles to your already heavy heart. Stop worrying about things that are not for you to worry about and get some rest for the night. You will be needed back at the abbey just after the sun rises.

The Queen then rose back to her full height. Before walking away, she forced a fleeting polite smile down below to Merlin. He felt a wave of sadness rush through him; there was a pounding in his temples. With a sigh, he retired for the evening.

The next afternoon, after tending to his patients in the abbey, Merlin set himself to exploring the keep and the castle grounds. He told himself this was important work—he spent too much of his time in forests and not enough inside these fortress walls where King Arthur and his knights would be penned in during a prolonged siege. How would he know how to help them if he had never familiarized himself with the castle's interiors.

He strolled through the lower floors of the central keep, making careful mental notes of each room. Nobody bothered him; the servants retreated at his approach, anxiously crossing themselves. Despite the initial success of his endeavor—he had made a superb mental catalog of the bottom three floors—Merlin felt listless and disappointed. Everything he observed—bedrooms, storerooms, armories, a small library, kitchen, pantry, great and minor halls—struck him as worn and sluggish. His legs were impatient to move, and he wanted to find something, but he was not sure what it was.

On to the fourth floor he went to King Arthur's apartments, which were shared with the King's most esteemed knights. There was a heap of scabbards, swords, daggers, and helmets in one room, all streaked with dirt, blood, and stray bits of reddish-pink soft innards.

The next room contained an even bigger pile, but this one had animal hides and boar tusks and stag horns. While the blood and organs had been carefully cleaned away, Merlin still smelled the foul odor of recent death. He had to leave quickly before he vomited.

He was reminded of the first time he saw a dead animal, when he was a small boy walking in the forests north of Logres. It was a dead bird that had fallen from a tree branch. He did not understand why it was lying motionless and stiff with its eyes wide open. He tried to prod it to get up and fly again, but the bird would not respond.

A kindly fairy, a dear old friend of his father, bent over him and explained the bird was dead.

He asked her: What is dead?

She told him: Dead is when you cannot move or see or hear or speak.

He asked if he would also die one day. She answered: I do not know. Fairies do not die, and you are part fairy. Humans die, and you are part human.

He decided he could inventory Arthur's apartments another time. He trudged up the last staircase, wheezing from exhaustion. These were Guinevere's rooms, quiet, tranquil, and devoid of people. He wandered about the Queen's apartments until he came upon several baskets filled with crumpled gowns, wrinkled, smudged, and ready to be washed. But one basket was different, not in the way it looked, but in its smell. The lady who had worn that gown must have applied far too much perfume because the lavender scent still clung tightly to her clothes.

Suddenly feeling how tired his limbs were, Merlin buried his face in that lavender-scented gown. His nagging restlessness and disappointment faded away, and he experienced a warm glow as if he were in a safe shelter, by a blazing hearth, during a raging thunderstorm. His eyes closed, his muscles relaxed, and he was soon in a deep sleep.

High-pitched screams and kicks in his ribs woke Merlin. He pulled his head up, dripping with saliva, and rubbed the sleep from his eyes. It was twilight—he must have slept for hours—and some handmaidens had returned to the Queen's apartments, clearly unhappy to find him where he did not belong.

Without speaking a word, Merlin scampered away and down the stairs as fast as he could go. He rushed away from the keep and through the castle courtyard. The guards stopped him at the gates, but when their captain saw it was Merlin the Enchanter, he let him pass without any questions.

Striding past the abbey, he heard the monks loudly chanting the evening Mass. He cringed. They and their faith should have stayed far away in—where was it their god had suffered his torments?—Yes, Jerusalem, stayed in Jerusalem, in whatever distant land that was. Merlin imagined Jerusalem as a city with no trees, but many angry, humorless men shrilly speaking Latin and crossing themselves. An impossibly remote place, but somehow its emissaries, brought by the old Romans, had traveled to these distant islands and would not let the fairies be at peace in their forests and hills.

He kept walking until he reached the forest, where he thankfully could no longer hear the Latin hymns. Although the sun was setting, his eyes could see easily in the dark, and his feet instinctively knew where to step. And soon he heard another song, not in Latin, but in the common tongue of Logres, a peasant song about harvests and moons, sung by a woman.

Merlin followed the sound to a lake, which reflected the dark pink light of the twilight sky. On the water's edge, squatting down in the tall grass, was a young maiden. He recognized her—she was the lovely girl with the long red hair.

He approached her stealthily. He stared longingly at her, relieved there was no one else present to observe and scold him. But as the darkness crept over the lake, her singing stopped and she stood up, looking suddenly quite worried.

Merlin spoke to her: Are you lost, my lady?

She jumped back when she saw him and crossed herself.

There is no need to be scared of me, he continued, I am very short, very stiff in my limbs, and very old. But there are other things you should be scared of in this forest, things animal and spirit and maybe even human that would take joy from hurting a pretty maiden like yourself. Take my hand, I know the way, I can lead you back to the castle.

Hesitating for a moment, she looked up at the black sky, with only a tiny sliver of a moon, and she looked to the side into the impenetrable darkness between the wide tree trunks. Then she took his hand.

Merlin led her slowly and carefully through the forest, cautioning her about approaching rocks, streams, and various crawling and slithering things in the dirt that could bite her. They spoke further as they traveled:

What is your name, my lady?

Viviane.

And where are you from Lady Viviane? Are you a daughter of one of the lords of Logres?

She sighed, as if she were stifling some strong feeling in her heart, and then answered: My father was a liege lord of King Arthur. He held the fortress halfway between here and Carduel. He died when I was a baby—a Saxon archer picked him off while he was walking along the ramparts. My brother looks after me, he is much older and he is a knight—

although he is not famous. But he is a good man. We came for the tournament.

Merlin mumbled an incantation, and, with his free hand, pulled a small herb from his belt and noisily chewed and spit it out.

My Lord Merlin, are you unwell? Should we rest?

Aha! Yes! Your brother is Sir P____, the White Knight of the Frozen Lake—it was at a frozen lake near a fortress between here and Carduel that the White Knight fought off a group of bandits. Your brother was wounded at the tournament, deep gash from a lance thrust into his left thigh. It took me some effort to get the spear point out of him. But he is healed now, and I sent him back to the castle. He is waiting for you, no doubt.

Viviane stopped walking and let go of his hand. How did you know so many things I did not tell you?

I am Merlin the Enchanter. I am King Arthur's seer. To be a seer, you must be able to see things. Don't look so frightened. The rumors that I know everything said and done in the past—and everything that will come to pass in the future—are foolishness. I can only see what the old gods of the forests and the rivers let me see, and I can only see it in brief flashes when I concentrate hard and harness my gift. Because I know your brother—because I have healed his wounds—it was easy for me to see his relation to you. Yet there are things I wish to see but I cannot. I have tried many times to see if I will die, but I always fail.

Merlin now felt ashamed at having said too much. He had never spoken before of his fear of death, but he had felt an inexplicable sudden compulsion to unburden his heart to Viviane. He longed for her to offer a kind word in response.

Please, take my hand again. Look around you—can you see where you are going in the dark night?

She took his hand once more without further protest, and the two walked quietly through the forest. They soon reached the meadow, not far from the abbey. As the way back to the castle was clear now, Viviane let go of his hand. Merlin wished her a good evening.

Aren't you returning to the castle? Are you not the King's guest at the banquet each evening?

No, I prefer the company of the owls tonight.

Viviane nodded, and walked briskly to the castle gates. Merlin watched her cross the meadow, marveling at her graceful bearing. He saw her pause before the guards and have some sort of discussion before they let her inside, and she disappeared from view.

He walked back to the lake in the forest where he had found Viviane singing earlier in the evening. He lay down on the patch of grass where she had sat, with his head turned up to the sliver of a moon in the night sky. He felt something near him on the ground and picked it up. It was a piece of fabric—torn from her dress? The fabric smelled like her skin smelled, so he was sure this was from her dress. He gripped it tightly.

Merlin inhaled a deep breath, full of familiar, soothing forest scents. For the first time in many days he was happy.

# III. The Nun's Rebuke

SO THERE YOU are, my dear old friend Merlin. I somehow knew you would grow tired of warm beds and make your way back to the twigs and the grass.

Merlin sat up and rubbed his eyes. It was morning, with a bright sun glaring overhead; he had slept for many hours. High above him, seated atop an immense horse, was King Arthur flanked by several knights and squires.

Come now, lads, help my Lord Merlin to his feet and don't mind the smell.

A pair of young men dismounted, helped Merlin up, dusted him off, and placed him on Arthur's horse. The King then returned Merlin to the abbey to resume his work as a healer.

On the way Merlin asked about the Lady Viviane.

Is that what drove you out to the woods? She is an orphan, little wealth in her family. Her brother will marry her off to someone suitable. If you are in need of a woman, let me know and I will find one for you. But I cannot have you distracted by this kind of nonsense.

Merlin assured Arthur that he would assist the King however he could, as he always had done. But Merlin did not take up the offer to be provided a woman. He did not want a bedmate to relieve his urges. No, he wanted to sit with Viviane in a corner of the forest far away from monks and knights and unburden his heart. He was sure she would listen patiently and kindly, and then draw his weary old head with plump warm tears stuck in his tangled beard upon her lap, and sing a sweet song.

Now that he knew her name, Merlin was able to use seeing spells to locate Viviane. He would eagerly go to wherever she was and make any conversation that he could—about the seasons, about the trees, about Arthur's youthful battles. She would answer politely and nervously. She never pushed him away, but, he also noticed, she never invited him to spend more time with her or asked him any questions.

Viviane was at all times accompanied by the same nun. She crossed herself and muttered in Latin whenever Merlin approached Viviane. Yet the nun drew back when he came near, and she did not try to stop their conversations.

He noticed, though, that with each passing day, Viviane's health declined. Her eyes grew bloodshot and puffy, her cheeks hollowed, her body quaked, and she hacked out dry, rattling coughs. Merlin asked if she was having difficulty resting at night. She blushed and stammered, but eventually admitted she was not sleeping well.

That is the cause of your sickness, he said, lack of sleep. Once you are able to sleep soundly, your ailments will disappear. I can mix you a warm brew that will help you rest at night: lavender, chamomile, honey, and valerian root.

But Viviane lurched away from him and shouted: No! I won't touch your potions. You are filthy. You are disgusting. You will not take my maidenhood with your sorcerer's tricks.

She ran off, out of his eyesight. Merlin was dumbfounded. Unsure what else to do, he went back to the woods to engage in awkward, idle banter with the birds and to try to lose the feeling of having committed some awful offense, even though he was at a loss as to what wrong he had done to the Lady Viviane.

The next morning, he discharged his final patients from the abbey. Happy to be done with the miserable monks who were forever cursing him, Merlin longed to see Viviane to seek forgiveness for whatever his mysterious transgression had been. But when he worked his spell, he could not see her location. He tried again and yet again once more, but all to no avail.

Confused and worried, Merlin hurried into the keep and up the stone stairs to the room where Viviane had been staying. But there were no traces anymore of Viviane or her brother. He only found the same angry nun, who was packing up some kind of bundle or other.

He asked where the Lady Viviane had gone.

The nun put down her bundle. She stood up very straight, rising slightly above Merlin's short, squat body. Tightly gripping the crucifix around her neck, she answered him shaking with fury:

You filthy lecherous heathen beast, you will stay away from the good, chaste Lady Viviane. She is revolted by your pagan ways, by your denial of the One True God and His Son and eternal salvation. Many good Christians say your father was a demon who forced himself on your mother—and I fully believe it. Your tricks and your conjuring are not the product of anything holy, but of dark, evil powers with which you have made some terrible pact. Son of a demon, worshipper of idols and fiends, harnesser of the devil's sorcery: Nothing good can come from you.

How many years has it been since you left your hole in the forest to come to Logres and whisper in the ears of kings? Decades? And in all that time, despite meeting countless bishops and monks and priests of the Holy Church, you have stubbornly refused to be baptized. You have heard of the wonders and the passion of Our Lord Jesus Christ; you have learned about the miracles He performed, and yet you still refuse to accept Him as your Savior and to embrace His Gospel. What can more clearly show the rot and wickedness in your heart?

Bad enough that you have poisoned the minds of kings and knights with your counsel, but at least they were grown men able to defend themselves. Now, though, you would molest an innocent maiden. I suppose that figures. Your father was a demon filled with lust and hatred of all things good and chaste, and so he forced himself upon your innocent mother, siring you. Like father, like son, your terrible hellish lusts have taken possession of you. But you will not harm the Lady Viviane. I found a Christian in a nearby village who once was a priest of your vile heathen faith, until his liege lord, fed up with this man's evil ways, made him choose between baptism and beheading. This Christian is not a particularly virtuous man; he makes a fool of himself drinking at the tavern. But he is a Christian and to help the Church he taught me a spell to make her invisible to your second sight. She has fled far away, and you will not find her. Do not think about her anymore, but think instead upon your many sins, embrace Our Savior, and repent while you still can, before this life ends and you face eternal judgment for your crimes.

Merlin was not upset by the nun's words. This was not the first scolding he had received from an official of the Church, and he had long grown indifferent to their passionate rages. Their powers were ultimately feeble on his native soil. The man whom the nun had trusted for her enchantment was a broken drunkard who continued to love the old gods and could not bear the emptiness of a world without their presence. That former pagan priest walked the forests still, but the fairies would no longer speak to him. He was so lonely with the Christian God, Who never came to comfort him, but preferred to judge him for his many sins in His distant court far away in the Christian Heaven.

This former pagan priest, Merlin realized, had tricked the nun: The man only knew how to block the second sight for short periods. Soon he would be able to see his beloved again. Still, he replied gently to the nun's wrath, as he worried about her influence upon Viviane:

Sister, I fear you are judging me falsely. I have no wish to harm the Lady Viviane. I perceived that she was falling ill from lack of sleep, and so I offered her medicine to help her rest and heal. The herbs I suggested are not aphrodisiacs. They relax the nerves to ease the way to sleep. I am fond of the girl, yes, but I do not have any dishonorable intentions. I am trying to help her, just as I helped her brother to heal from his wounds at the tournament.

But these words only infuriated the nun further:

You speak the lying words of the devil, of every evil tempter. What kind of a man stares the way you do at the Lady Viviane if he is not a slave to his filthy lusts? How can there be any doubt of your wicked intentions?

You say, with such feigned sincerity, that you wish only for the Lady Viviane's good health. But you are the sickness. She cannot sleep because of her terror that you will come into her room at night to take her maidenhood by force or by trickery. Even if we attempt to guard her bed against you, we know your demon powers permit you to change your shape and appear in the guise of anyone whom you wish to pretend to be. You could assume the shape of her brother, or her dead father, or the most handsome knight at the tournament, or King Arthur, or even me. How is the Lady Viviane to know who is her friend and who is a conjurer's trick? Poor girl, in her dread she stayed awake all night, jumping at the slightest sound, constantly on the watch for your sorcery.

Don't look at me with those baffled, innocent eyes. You have tricked and shamed other noble ladies before. When you were challenged to prove Arthur's right to the throne, you admitted—no, you boasted—of how you treacherously dishonored the good Lady Igraine. She was a faithful wife to the Duke of Tintagel. When King Uther Pendragon, overcome by his filthy lusts, stared at her across his great hall, she covered her face in shame and found pretexts to flee from his disgusting leering eyes.

And then Uther sought your counsel. He should have sought guidance from His Holiness the Bishop, who could have guided his heart back to Christ, to contrition and to chastity. But instead, King Uther went to you as his trusted adviser. And you did nothing to dissuade him from his sinful desires. No, you encouraged him. You plotted, with your sorcery to take Igraine's honor by vile trickery. You waited for the Duke to leave his wife alone in a castle, and then you used your magic, the magic you learned from demons, to make Uther appear as if he were the Duke of Tintagel. And you made yourself appear in the guise of the Duke's closest friend and adviser, so you could accompany your King.

You stood there, in the Castle of Tintagel, in the Lady Igraine's bedchamber, watching her fornicate with Uther Pendragon, knowing it was your enchantment that had tricked her into believing she was lying with her lawful husband. What were you thinking in your heathen mind when you watched Uther shame Igraine with the aid of your spell? While you stood there watching him take his pleasure, humiliating her, did you try to stop what was happening?

King Arthur was the issue of that night of black magic. And when he came of age and you wanted him on the throne of Logres, you openly boasted of these events to prove that Arthur was a man of high birth and Uther's rightful heir.

Can you not understand why the Lady Viviane was so frightened of you? You had no fear of God's law when Igraine was shamed. And you did not care that she was the wife of a great lord with his own army and castles. So what would you not stoop to do to an orphan girl, who has no husband or father, no armies and castles, to protect her?

# IV. How the Wizard Fell from Grace

MERLIN'S MOTHER HAD been a carefree, dreamy shepherdess in the countryside of Northumbria. As she later told the tale to her son, one day she wandered into the forest and met a handsome man. He was not young, but he was not old either. He had thick red hair that fell loosely below his broad shoulders, a red beard, and red eyes. This man was dressed simply in a rough linen tunic, although he smelled of flowers and dew. He asked what had brought her so far into the woods—was she not terrified that wild boars would attack her, or that she would be ravaged by heathen brutes who had not been baptized.

I followed the birds, she replied, I want to sing with them, if only I could understand what they were saying.

The handsome man sat down on a boulder. As soon as he rested his hands on the stone, dark green moss sprouted and rapidly covered the entire surface. He looked up towards the tree tops and sang a brief, beautiful song with no words. Down then came all the birds, robins and doves and blackbirds and sparrows and the rest. They perched on the boulder with the red-haired man and started singing and cooing all at the same time. But when he made a gesture for quiet, they immediately obeyed.

My dear lady, do you know the language of the birds?

No, I did not know the birds had a language.

Of course the birds have a language. As do the bees, and the butterflies, and the foxes, and the rabbits, and even the wind and the leaves. The people here once knew these things. But now the Christian priests fill your ears with the angry words of their god, who is so enraged at everything, who thinks everyone must beg His forgiveness for the crime of being born and wanting the simple pleasures all living things want. Once the people became so twisted with guilt and accusation, the birds and the beasts stopped wanting to speak to them. But you have no fear or shame, which is good. Do you want to learn how to speak to the creatures in this forest?

Very much so.

And so for the rest of that afternoon Merlin's mother neglected her flock of sheep and lingered deep in the woods, where her new friend taught her the language of the birds. After the sun fell from the sky, he led her out of the forest. When she arrived back home, her parents and sisters battered her with questions—where had she been, didn't she realize they had been forced to run around madly at dusk to round up her flock, didn't she know the lord could have accused them of stealing his sheep—but she found it hard to care about their worries. Mostly she was sad to no longer hear the pretty language of the birds.

Her parents told her she could not eat dinner until she explained what she had been doing all afternoon. Merlin's mother looked at her sisters wolfing down a stew of pigeon meat. After having chatted and sung so merrily with the birds that day, she was suddenly horrified that her parents had murdered such sweet creatures in order to eat them. Without further word, she strode back outside with the family's new round of indignant curses trailing after her.

She walked past the pen where the sheep were held for the night, past the big lazy guard dog, and into the wide open meadow nearby. She lay down on the grass and stared up at the stars and the moon. After a while, her belly ached with hunger. But rather than returning home, as she would have done before, to profusely apologize, this night she boldly called out to the birds, in their language, and asked for something to eat. And the birds came to her aid, bringing her a great feast of fruits and herbs.

From then on, Merlin's mother could not bear the company of her family or her fellow villagers. Each day she would slip away into the deep forest, to the spring close to where she had first met the handsome red-headed man. She would find the boulder that he had covered with moss, sit on it, and wait for him to come to her. Some days he arrived soon after her, and some days he took a little longer. But when he came, he was always kind and taught her some new wonder—another creature's language, or the healing powers of different plants. He showed her fruits and herbs that satisfied her appetite so well that she no longer wished to eat meat or drink milk.

Her parents complained loudly and often about their daughter's ever longer absences. They dragged her to the village church and locked her into a room with the priest. This priest, a lanky, withered beanpole with no hair on his head or face, railed at her about humanity's sinful nature and how salvation was only possible through the redemptive, unspeakably awful sufferings that the Savior had undergone on the cross on her behalf.

She had been seen going into the woods, day after day, and remaining there for hours. Was she meeting a man? Or a devil? Was she fornicating with him? Did she not realize that fornication was a terrible sin, that such fleeting pleasure of the gross, dirty flesh would damn her soul to eternal suffering in the next life?

The priest's words bounced off her like pebbles tossed against an old sturdy oak tree. As the priest's small bald head grew redder and his voice became louder, Merlin's mother felt intolerably bored. Seeing no point in trying to speak to this angry man, she sighed and sang a pretty song that the blackbirds had taught her. The priest now crossed himself furiously, threw holy water at her head, and switched his screaming from the common tongue to Latin.

Finally, the priest let her go. He told her parents that either she was possessed by a devil or she was fornicating with one. They rent their hair, sobbed, and begged her to confess her sins and to seek absolution from the Holy Church. Fed up with these silly hysterics over her lovely times in the woods with the wonderful creatures and the kind man, she walked away, determined to leave the village forevermore.

It was already early evening when she came to the spring and the moss-covered rock. The handsome red-haired man asked why she had entered the woods so late. She recounted what had happened and beseeched him to let her live with him in the forest.

And then, on a sudden impulse, she added: If you will make me your bride, I will pledge my love to you eternally.

In response, he leaned down, kissed her lips, and then led her deeper into the forest, until they came to a hill. He placed his hands on a patch of grass, revealing a hidden door. She followed him inside, into a huge, brightly lit indoor palace with blue marble floors and ceilings and tables laid with sumptuous baskets of fruits and vegetables. There were fairies flitting about on their silver wings, each about the half the size of a grown human woman.

The red-haired man led her through winding corridors until she came to a bed surrounded by a canopy made from leaves and vines. That night he lay with her and sired upon her a baby boy, whom she named Merlin.

Merlin grew up in the deep woods and the fairies' Otherworld palace concealed within the enchanted hill. He was a prodigy: He could already speak when he was born, both human and animal languages, and he was up and walking in only a few weeks. He reached his full adult height at the age of three, although he was of a short stature—barely bigger than the fairies buzzing about.

The fairies taught him to use herbs and spells to heal the sick and the wounded, and how to cast charms that would permit him to see the past and the future and events that were far away. When he was a little boy, Merlin often followed the fairies on their rounds to tend to the flower blooms or to assist the bees in brewing their honey, which their grateful and chivalrous queens would magnanimously share.

And so Merlin lived happily for the first ten years of his life, until the idyll ended abruptly one morning. It was the loudest morning of Merlin's then brief life: screeching horses—many screeching horses—were complaining bitterly of their heavy burdens and the sharp pains of spurs grinding into their sides. On top of the horses' moans were the sounds of metal clanking and banging, and human voices yelling at each other about a boy they were looking for in the forest.

Merlin sat up and rubbed the sleep from his eyes. He had been lying in the grass in a small clearing, next to a pond. A frog hopped onto his lap, wished him a hearty good morning, and then went off about his business. He tried to figure out who these loud people encased in metal were searching for. Had somebody become lost in the woods? He did not remember seeing any boy who had lost his way.

The voices grew louder and approached closer. Suddenly Merlin found himself surrounded by three horses. One man, who was not clad in metal, said: That is him. And then another man in armor grabbed the boy by his hair and pulled him up onto his horse.

The horses rode quickly out of the forest. Merlin started to cry, but his sobs only got him a vicious smack from a metal glove. After the group of men had cleared the woods and entered a broad meadow, they stopped and dismounted. They bound Merlin's feet and hands and locked him in a cage in the back of a wagon. Then the group set out again, riding on until they reached a castle.

There was a wide clearing in front of the fortress walls, filled with scattered porous black rocks, and beyond them was a moat of brackish water that stank of sewage. The perfectly rectangular chiseled grey stones of the castle walls lacked even a single vine or bird's nest to lend them an air of gentleness.

One of the armed men on horseback shouted something indistinct to the guards on the ramparts, who responded by lowering the gate so they could cross over the moat. The courtyard of the stronghold was more grey stone, splattered with the blood of freshly killed animals, to judge from the carcasses swinging nearby. There were many men and women bustling about and getting upset with each other. Merlin called out to a sad looking cow in a pen and asked her what this place was, but the cow only moaned back that she could not bear how much it had pained her to watch the man cut her baby's neck and skin the calf's hide in front of her very eyes.

Merlin was dragged through high wooden doors into a large building, then down a short corridor, and into an enormous room packed with a great assembly of strange people. He was brought before a man sitting at the head of a grand table and thrown at his feet.

This man—to whom the others showed deference—grabbed Merlin's shoulder and told him to stand up straight. Then he turned his head to a group of twelve men in hooded cloaks and asked them if this was the right boy.

After a pause, an older man in a hooded cloak answered: Your Grace, King Vortigern, this is the boy. If you wish your tower to stand we need his blood, the blood of the demon child.

How much blood? Vortigern asked. Can we prick him a little, or do you need more?

We need all of it, Sire. It is a large tower. He will need to be drained in full.

Merlin had by now recovered from his initial shock and realized the danger he was in. Thinking quickly, he mumbled a spell. There was a loud thunderclap in Vortigern's hall, and for an instant, the room was filled with trees that just as quickly vanished into thin air. This marvel silenced Vortigern and the hooded men.

Then Merlin spoke: They are liars, King Vortigern. My blood will be of no help to you. Only I know why your tower does not stand. Treat me like a proper guest and I may deign to tell you the secret. These men fear me because they fear I will tell you the truth and expose their ignorance.

The leader of the hooded men stepped forward again to respond: Your Grace, do not listen to him—he is an evil creature, the child of the Devil. We examined the stars and plotted their course, and we cast our dice with the sacred runes upon them, and the signs were unmistakable: The blood of the boy sired by a demon is the only way. There have been rumors for years of such a monster roaming the forests, forcing good Christians to cross themselves when they pass through the woods, and now we have captured him. Let's be done with him—his blood to reinforce the tower so it will stand, and the unchristian abomination con-signed back to his father in Hell.

Merlin felt his initial fear turn to rage: King Vortigern, these men are liars. My father is no demon.

Vortigern leaned back in his chair and looked first at the hooded men, then at Merlin. He snorted and hummed tune-lessly to himself. He struck Merlin as bizarrely calm—this man was weighing whether to kill him, but he seemed as if he were deciding whether he preferred sunrises or sunsets. Eventually he asked Merlin a question: Boy, do you live in the forest?

Yes, I do, King Vortigern.

And who are your parents?

My mother is named A____, from the village of W_____, in Northumbria. My father is from the Otherworld, the realm of the fairies, and he looks after the forest and all who dwell there—birds, bees, beasts, even fairies. But he is no demon.

The leader of the hooded men now jumped forward and pointed a bony forefinger at Merlin's forehead, almost touching him: See, Your Grace, his father is a demon. If not human, and if not angel, then what else could he be?

Vortigern, still appearing quite calm, turned back to Merlin again: Boy that was quite a marvel you showed us, with the thunder and the vanishing trees. Did your father teach you that trick?

Merlin smiled as he grasped his path to safety: King Vortigern, my father gifted me with certain abilities, and the fairies taught me their secret wisdom. You have seen only a small speck of what I can conjure. Free me from being your prisoner, make me your guest and guarantee my safety, and I will show you wonders. I can even show you why your tower will not stand.

Eh, and why is that?

First feed me and lock up the wicked men who wish to kill me. Then let me rest properly, and I shall tell you.

Vortigern turned his eyes back to the hooded men and asked them: Can any of you make the thunder sound in this hall, or summon trees and make them disappear?

These are unchristian, evil tricks, Your Grace, you must not heed them. We will not stoop to such dark magic.

The King took a drink from his goblet of wine. He looked up at the high ceiling of his great hall and scrunched up his face in an exaggerated expression of deep thought. After a few moments of silence, Vortigern ordered his guards to seize the hooded men and lock them up.

Once they were gone he asked the boy for his name.

Sire, it is Merlin.

Well, Merlin, this man here—and he pointed to a man at his side—is a steward of mine. He will take you to your room in the keep and get you fed and washed. Tomorrow you shall tell me why my tower cannot stand.

Later that night, alone in his small room, Merlin uttered a series of incantations for a seeing spell. The work was diffi-cult, as outside the forest it was harder to harness the spirits of the fairy Otherworld. But with persistence he was able to summon the visions he sought.

As best he could discern from the fleeting, choppy im-ages and snippets of sounds, Vortigern kept building a tower in a particular spot, but it would invariably collapse on its side into a heap of debris. The location must have had some unusual importance, for otherwise Merlin could not figure out why the King would not simply move the structure somewhere else.

Vortigern had summoned his court astrologers and demanded that they tell him how to make the tower stand. These sages had then studied and charted the stars and studied some more, and conjured spirits, and cast runes, but all to no avail; they had no idea why the tower fell. Merlin saw them gesture angrily at each other, and they appeared to be shouting—perhaps they had turned on each other in frustration.

Then another image revealed itself to his mind. Their leader, the eldest astrologer, was casting his own horoscope. Merlin surmised he must have been worried about the King's reaction to their failure. Those calculations and charts showed that the astrologers would die soon at the hands of a boy in the forest whose father was not a mortal man. Merlin now realized why he had been kidnapped: They had tried to save themselves by concocting the lie that the only way to make the tower stand was to murder him and use his blood to reinforce the structure.

The puzzle of the falling tower was harder to unravel. Several times he watched the tower fall in his visions, but saw nothing that caused the collapse. Deducing that there must be something underneath the foundation that was jostling the stones, Merlin summoned the spirits of the water that runs deep under the ground and asked them to show him what they could see. With their aid, he understood the problem and grasped the solution.

The next morning, at Merlin's request, King Vortigern brought him to the site of the crumbled tower. He instructed Vortigern's men to clear the rubble from the base of the tower and dig deeply into the ground below. They dug until they reached a shallow underground pool.

Drain the water, Merlin said. And they did so, revealing two stone slabs.

Remove the slabs, Merlin said. And they did so.

But when the stones were gone, the workmen shrieked in terror and ran scrambling in all directions.

Merlin told King Vortigern to ignore the commotion, and rather to watch the sky. They soon heard booming groans, and then two dragons soared into the air from the open pit.

There was a white dragon and a red dragon, and they fought each other viciously, with terrible moans that were louder than thunder claps. Eventually the red dragon broke free of the grip of the white dragon, flew above its enemy's head, and then breathed fire down upon him, quickly reducing his rival to a pile of ashes. In triumph the red dragon flew away, across the meadow, over the forest, until he finally disappeared between faraway mountain peaks.

King Vortigern asked Merlin what was the meaning of these wonders.

Your Grace, he answered, unlike your astrologers who lied to you and attempted to murder me, I will tell the truth. I could see only so much in my visions. I saw that the dragons must be freed to let your tower stand, but nothing more was revealed to me.

Vortigern nodded his approval and ordered his men to rebuild the tower. He returned to his hall with Merlin in tow. Once back, the King had his gaggle of hooded wise men summarily executed, both for their incompetence and for their treacherous lies.

Merlin now politely asked leave to return to his home in the forest. But King Vortigern refused: the enchanter's skills were too valuable to relinquish. And even if he were willing to forego using Merlin's gifts himself, he could not risk the wizard falling into the hands of his enemies and being put to use by them. So Merlin would have to remain as Vortigern's guest—an esteemed guest who would be afforded every comfort and luxury.

Looking out the windows at the high ramparts, and around the room at the rows of men in chainmail with dangling swords, Merlin heaved a sigh and resigned himself to being where he was for the time being.

Days passed, then weeks, months, and several years. At first, Merlin was sad to be exiled to this violent world of fortresses and knights, and would keep to himself in his room unless he was summoned by Vortigern or needed to eat. But his reticence soon faded away as Merlin discovered the pleasures of exalted rank.

When Vortigern would summon him, the courtiers and knights would cease their conversations and step back deferentially to let the short, stumpy enchanter walk to the King's seat. Vortigern would ask him if he had seen the movements of the Saxon raiding parties, or how the harvest would go, or if some lord were plotting against him. Sometimes Merlin knew the answer from visions he had already seen, while other times he had to retire to his room to recite incantations to place himself into a trance in which events of the past or the future or the faraway present could be perceived clearly. But either way, Merlin's visions always proved true.

Vortigern granted leave to Merlin to collect herbs for medicines and spells in the woods near the castle as long as he was escorted by an armed guard of loyal men; no doubt, the King said, Merlin's fame would attract greedy kidnappers. With these herbs, Merlin was able to work as a healer as well as a seer, tending to the many wounds of the knights and the illnesses of children and the old. His healing powers only made him more feared and admired.

The knights of Vortigern's court jostled and connived to be detailed to protect Merlin on his trips to the nearby forests. Out in the woods, they would privately petition him to intervene on their behalf in some matter with the King, as His Grace listened to no one's counsel more closely than that of the diminutive wizard.

And Merlin was always eager to help. He cared little about the substance of the requests—disputes about land boundaries or inheritance or marriage arrangements—but he reveled in the look of submissive gratitude in the eyes of the noble courtiers. The more men he aided, the more men in the court were keen to please and accommodate him. He heard many words of flattery, and despite his better judgment, these praises did have a way of seeping into his heart.

Yet not all was well. The Christian priests loathed Merlin, convinced he was the Devil's son and that his visions and medicines were traps set by Lucifer to lure Christians away from their faith into a trust in dark magic. But the clerics' scolding words were largely ignored: If an enemy thrust a spear deep into a knight's thigh, it was Merlin's ointments and spells, not the priests' sermons, that eased the pain and healed the wound.

It was worse with the women of the court. As Merlin grew into manhood, he yearned for women who least resembled the fairies in the woods: tall, refined noble ladies who wore elegant gowns and disdained outdoor pursuits. These women were also often the most pious Christians, preferring edifying tracts about holy saints and martyrs to hunts or tournaments.

Merlin's love was always unrequited. In the heady rush of passion, he would fall at the feet of his beloved, a rumpled little ball of plump bluish flesh and knotted, dirty hair and declare his eternal devotion and passionate love. The kinder ladies would gently ask him to rise, thank him coldly for his generous praises, which they swore they did not deserve, but with a forced and artificial sigh, regretfully inform Merlin that their hearts had been already carried away by another—if only he had been there sooner perhaps it would be different, but what has happened cannot be undone, and love has its own logic.

The less kind ladies shrieked that he was a demon sent to lure them into perdition and damnation. One or two even beat him away with a broom and threw small wooden crosses at his back as he fled in humiliation.

After each failed profession of love Merlin would rush back to his room in Vortigern's keep, close the shutters, and bury his face in his thick woolen blanket to muffle the sound of sobs so violent that his body quaked and sometimes tumbled over. Terrible visions came to him at these moments—men hacking their families apart with pick axes, savage wolves tearing the flesh off a sheep, or hot lava pouring rapidly down a mountainside into a city, melting and burning all the houses and people in its path.

When he had calmed down again, he would firmly resolve to stop shaming himself before the prim, unattainable ladies of the court. They looked at him with pity or disgust, but never desire. He realized in these moments of clarity that they could never feel passion for him, so short, so ugly, so heathen. The graceful ladies gave their love to the towering muscular knights of the Christian court, and that was simply the way the world was. He told himself to accept that they desired what they desired. Accept, and renounce these humiliating infatuations.

But he could not do so. Like a bucket tethered to a well, Merlin's heart went through a never-ending cycle of being filled and emptied. When empty, he could see clearly how foolishly he had behaved. Yet, soon again there would be a banquet. Merlin would be seated in a place of honor, next to His Grace, King Vortigern. He would feel powerful and esteemed. He would have just finished counseling the King on an important matter, and perhaps earlier in the day he had been showered with blessings by a mother whose child he had cured of a raging fever. With these praises humming in his ears, Merlin would forget he was a misshapen little man with a tangled unkempt beard, and he would begin to feel that he belonged in the court, as if born to it like the tall strapping knights around him.

In the half-light of the candles placed around the horseshoe-shaped table, Merlin, drunk with smug pride, would look about the hall, taking in the joyful scene—elegant clothes, smiling tipsy faces, the sounds of cups clinking and funny anecdotes being exchanged, even a risqué ballad. And then he would catch sight of a woman smiling and leaning into a friend to say something that made them both laugh. Her dress would fit her body perfectly, as if it had grown naturally from her skin. Her every gesture and expression would radiate a natural-born ease in her surroundings.

He would then notice something in particular about the way she looked. It could be her hair, soft, thick, and carefully styled. Or her eyes. Or her lips. Or her long slender legs. Whatever the feature was, Merlin would fixate upon it until the rest of the hall faded into a blurred background. That night he would dream of this woman, imagine her cradling his head gently and kissing him ardently, and when he woke he knew he was once more deliriously in love.

# V. How Merlin Counseled
# King Uther Pendragon

AND SO WENT Merlin's life at Vortigern's court until the day came when a breathless messenger arrived in the great hall to announce that Uther Pendragon, the brother of the King whom Vortigern had betrayed and overthrown, had landed off the coast with his army, determined to retake the crown of Logres. While Vortigern and his loyal barons scrambled to ready themselves for war, Merlin prepared to abandon his King. For he had actually known all along the meaning of the omen of the red dragon defeating the white dragon: that Uther the red dragon would vanquish and kill Vortigern the white dragon.

That night Merlin took advantage of the chaos caused by the panicked and sudden battle preparations to slip away into the forest. For three days he wandered merrily among the trees, picking fruits and herbs, and making idle chatter with the birds and the insects about the weather and such. He told himself that this was where he belonged, and that his life at the Christian court had been a strange hazy dream.

But on the morning of the fourth day, as he was watching the sun rise, he met a fairy whom he had known many years ago, in his boyhood. She said she had not expected to find him returned to the woods, after he had abandoned his family for so many years. She scolded him for using the forest's secrets to curry favor among the Christians. And then, with a bitter edge to her voice, she informed Merlin that, out of grief at his disappearance, his father had taken his mother far away from these lands to the Blessed Isle of Avalon, to eat the apples of forgetfulness and so lose the horrible pain of being abandoned by her only child.

And with that, the fairy stomped off.

Merlin sat down on a rock and pondered his situation. He felt a deep sadness at his mother's departure, but he could not bring himself to cry. Rather, he felt the sadness sit in his chest like a bad winter chill. He knew the fairy was right: He had abandoned his parents. He could have left Vortigern's castle long ago, once the guard detail had been loosened and he had gained permission to forage in the woods for fruits and herbs. And he had known for years that the day would come when Uther Pendragon would return and depose Vortigern.

So why had he lingered among the Christians in their stone towers? He mulled this question through the morning, although his mind was clouded by the sadness wedged inside him and the echoes of the fairy's harsh rebukes. But when the answer came with startling clarity, he felt even greater shame: He had lingered at the Christian court because that is what he had wanted to do. He had betrayed his family and the fairies and the creatures of the forest because he had enjoyed being cajoled, feared, and flattered by so many powerful men.

Remembering the thrill he had felt as barons quaked in fear when he leaned into King Vortigern's ear, the sorrow now lifted from Merlin's chest. Instead, he felt an overwhelming boredom at everything around him in the forest: The same big trees that looked alike, growing ever slightly taller each year; the same flowers and fruits, blossoming and withering in their never-varying cycle. But worst of all were the creatures of the woods. Many noblemen had said how they envied Merlin for his ability to speak to birds, beasts, and fish, apparently convinced that these beings knew deep, profound secrets. Yet nothing could be further from the truth: Birds were actually quite stupid, their minds fixated upon the weather and food. And the fish were even dumber.

Merlin no longer walked towards his native forests of Northumbria, but instead changed direction and proceeded to Uther's camp to offer his aid. Well-known as Vortigern's sorcerer, he was immediately taken prisoner and interrogated closely as to his whereabouts and intentions. From their questions, Uther's officers seemed to be convinced that Merlin was there to poison or enchant Vortigern's enemies. But through it all Merlin remained calm and repeated that he had no desire to harm Uther's cause.

Eventually Uther Pendragon himself summoned Merlin. When he met Uther, he was pleasantly surprised: Unlike the knights of Vortigern's court who were tall and muscular and reddish-blonde, Uther was short and squat with messes of unkempt brown curly hair on his head, face, neck, and ears.

Enchanter, Uther began, why are you here? You say you intend no harm, but you have still not said why you are here.

Your Grace, King Uther Pendragon, I am here because you are destined to be King. When I was first brought to Logres by Vortigern, I had him free two dragons trapped in the ground, the red dragon and the white dragon. They fought a terrible battle in the sky, but the red dragon prevailed. I told Vortigern that day that I could not read the meaning of the sign, but I lied to him because the truth would have cost me my head: You are the red dragon, and you will slaughter your foe, the white dragon, and reclaim your kingdom.

In four days' time, in the wide meadow outside of the Castle of L.___, your two armies will meet. The fighting will be fierce throughout the morning and neither side will be able to gain an advantage over the other. When the sun reaches its zenith in the sky, you will clearly see three clouds darken and become red dragons. These red dragons will sweep down into Vortigern's army to terrify his knights. At that moment your men will break his lines and crush the usurper.

Keep me prisoner here until the four days have passed. If matters have not come to pass as I predict, then do what you will with me. But if I have foretold your victory truthfully, then I ask you to acknowledge my wisdom and my second sight, and to take me into your service.

Uther Pendragon betrayed no emotion as Merlin spoke. As you wish, enchanter, was his only reply. Then Merlin was escorted away, clapped in chains, and forced to eat moldy black bread from a dish on the ground like an old dog. But he endured these humiliations serenely, confident his visions would prove true.

And so they did: Uther overcame his enemies precisely when and where Merlin had said he would, and everyone at the battle witnessed the marvel of the three phantom red dragons falling from the sky and frightening Vortigern's forces. After capturing and beheading Vortigern, Uther ordered Merlin's release and seated him in a place of honor at the celebratory banquets. Uther had many questions for his new court sorcerer, which Merlin answered as best he could from the visions he had seen. Merlin also took charge of the care of the soldiers wounded in the great battle, and he won over the hearts of Uther's followers by saving many knights from what had been feared to be a mortal wound or permanently crippling injury.

Once again, Merlin was feted and admired, and he rejoiced in the exercise of power. He did not grieve for the fallen Vortigern, or the defeated King's courtiers, forced to flee as their lands were confiscated and looted. Merlin was surprised at his cold heart, but he chose not to judge himself harshly: The omen of the two dragons showed that the shift in power had long been foreordained by the hidden spirits that weave the destiny of men, and Merlin's tears, had there been any, would have been a pitifully futile gesture.

Yet not all was well. At Christmastime, when the King hosted his nobles in his great hall, Merlin noticed that Uther was staring too hard and long at the party of the Duke of Tintagel, who were seated down the side of the large horseshoe table. He wondered why the King had this sudden, intense interest in the Duke—could the Duke be plotting treason? Had Uther learned something that Merlin had failed to see in his visions?

Merlin waited for an opportune moment to ask Uther what his worry was, but he did not cease from his agitated, intense staring. Perhaps it is a drunken stupor, Merlin thought, for the King cannot intend to make such an odd spectacle of himself in front of all his barons.

Eventually, Merlin felt compelled to gently intervene: Your Grace, it is late and you seem tired. Would you like to retire for the night?

Without moving his eyes or his head, Uther Pendragon only grunted in response, a sound that was a cross between snorting and sighing.

Merlin tried again: Your Grace, you may give the impression, with your glare, that you are angry with the Duke of Tintagel.

What? No! Never!

Uther now stood up, shouted across the table to the Duke, and urged him to come over. Once the Duke had crossed the room to join the King, Uther embraced him warmly, spoke of how much he valued the Duke's friendship, and insisted that the Duke and his wife, the noble Lady Igraine, accompany him the next morning for a ride through the woods.

After the Duke had returned to his seat, Uther turned back to Merlin. He would start to speak of one matter, but when Merlin would begin to answer him, the King would interrupt and launch into a different topic. Although he could not stay focused on any one point, the King spoke with giddy enthusiasm and his face was flush. His lips kept forming into a smile, and he seemed to radiate a bursting joyfulness.

The next morning Uther Pendragon went out riding with Duke Gorlois of Tintagel and his wife the Lady Igraine. Still concerned about the King's strange behavior at dinner, Merlin mounted the castle ramparts to watch them before they disappeared into the woods. They were an odd sight: Both Gorlois and Igraine were tall, slender, and powerfully built, with pale complexions and blonde hair, which was painfully bright in the sunshine. Uther looked absurd riding between them, a rumpled short mess of black curls and big pink pimples, with puddles of sweat soaking through his clothes. But once again, his face was flush with smiles and happiness.

They did not return to the castle for several hours. That evening, Uther chose to dine alone with Gorlois and Igraine. Merlin retired to his bed early in the hope that he could conjure a vision that perhaps could make sense of Uther's behavior. When the vision would not come, no matter how much he tried, he sighed and decided that sleep would do him good.

But shortly after midnight, Merlin was awoken by a loud banging on the door to his room. When he opened it, a royal page, who looked himself as if he had just been yanked from his sleep, informed Merlin that King Uther Pendragon had summoned him to an emergency meeting of his closest advisors. Merlin quickly dressed, splashed cold water on his face, and followed the page to the King's bedchamber.

There he found Uther pacing frantically about the room, his eyes bloodshot, and heaving sighs as his face moved back and forth between stupid grins and anguished frowns. Merlin could not tell if the King was joyful, gloomy, or mad. There were several other royal advisors present, muscular knights who had been the King's companions in many battles.

The page drowsily announced that the esteemed Lord Merlin was now present.

Excellent! Uther thundered. Excellent! Now we may begin.

After the page had made a discreet exit, and Uther had confirmed that he was alone with his advisors, the King confided he was suffering from a terrible sickness. His pulse was racing, his heart was palpitating, and his legs could not keep still. He felt both a tormented longing and a surging excitement. He seemed to be about to say something more, but then his face turned scarlet, and he resumed his silent pacing. None of his advisors spoke a word.

Finally, he stood still again and faced them. He looked at the ground, heaved a loud sigh, and closed his eyes. Then he announced, firmly but slowly: I am in love with the Lady Igraine. I cannot be apart from her. I must have her, I must embrace her. For so many years I spurned love as I focused all my might on seeking vengeance against Vortigern for murdering my brother and usurping our throne, but now that I am victorious, the old goddess of love has come for her revenge upon me. She has cursed me, and I do not know what to do.

Merlin spoke up first: Your Grace, you were wise to say you are suffering from a sickness. This passion you feel can bring you only dishonor. Igraine is married and a pious woman; she will never consent to lie with you. I have seen this sickness before, and it drives men to shameful acts. You must get away from her. Her face, her voice, it feeds your illness, tightens its grip on your chest and makes your brain rage with fever. The only cure is to go away and forget her. Surround yourself with other women, maidens who could make suitable brides. Once Your Grace is married, you will see how easy it is to douse these flames. And to lay with your lawful wife will not bring you into disrepute.

In response, Uther slumped down to the floor. He looked straight ahead, as if he were trying to make out something in the far distance. His eyes swelled with thick tears that tumbled down his face.

His other courtiers, the gallant knights of the court, now offered their counsel: Your Grace, the enchanter Merlin may be able to tell fortunes and heal wounds, but he is ignorant of love—has he ever won a lady's heart? While he means only to protect your honor, these matters are beyond his knowledge. We have all fought the battles of love and emerged victorious. Follow our advice—bestow lovely gifts upon Igraine, praise her beauty and wisdom, and then boldly declare your love to her. Once she sees how her charms have felled such a mighty King, she will not be so cruel as to refuse her favors to you.

The King stood up again and praised his knights for speaking wisely. Merlin, he continued, these intrigues are not for you. And with that, he dismissed Merlin from his presence.

For the next several days Uther Pendragon did not seek his counsel. Merlin saw him whispering excitedly with his knights or out in the meadows and woods riding with Duke Gorlois and Lady Igraine, whom he had detained long after the other lords and ladies had returned to their homes. From what Merlin could tell, the King appeared happy. Although he still worried that this adventure would turn out poorly, he began to doubt himself—maybe the handsome knights did know better about the strange ways of a woman's heart.

And this was how matters stood until Merlin was roughly dragged from his bed late one night by the King's seneschal to answer Uther Pendragon's urgent summons. When Merlin entered Uther's bed chamber, the King was sitting on the floor, shivering beneath dirty, wrinkled sheets. Several knights were pacing the room liked caged wolves, with a violent glare in their eyes and an aggressive edge to their restless movements.

The King jumped up and ran over to embrace him. Merlin, he shouted hoarsely, oh my dear Merlin, she has gone, she has run away from me. But you can see where she went, I am sure of it, you will find her for me, and then I can seize her and bring her back. Please, I beg you, do this for me. I cannot be parted from her.

But Merlin coldly replied: Your Grace, I cannot find whomever you seek unless you tell me her name and why she is fleeing.

Uther sank back down to the floor. After a couple of minutes of silence, he ordered everyone to leave the room except Merlin. Once they were alone, he told his tale:

After several days largely spent riding and eating with Gorlois and Igraine—days in which he had made what he thought were cleverly subtle and discreet praises of Igraine's beauty and wisdom—Uther had decided the time was right to declare his love. While she had not encouraged his interest, she had not pushed him away either, or at least not in any way that he had noticed. He consulted his knights, who were sure Igraine was ready to yield herself to the King if only he were to ask. They insisted that Igraine, like all women, was cunning in matters of the heart, and had no doubt fully grasped what he felt and desired; that she had not made a point of rebuffing him could mean only that she welcomed his attentions and was waiting for the invitation from him to consummate their shared passion.

Earlier that day, around twilight, his knights had persuaded Duke Gorlois to come with them to practice their charges against a target dummy set up in the meadow just beyond the fortress walls. With Igraine left by herself, he had slipped quietly into the room in the keep where the Duke's party had been staying. She gasped when she saw him, but he told her not to be alarmed. He then knelt down before his beloved—his knights had told him that ladies found this pose of supplication to be irresistible—and declared that she had vanquished his heart, how he loved only her, and could think of nothing else, day or night, except her beauty. And he begged her to grant him the favor of a tender embrace and a passionate kiss.

When Uther stood up again, so sure there would be soft, willing lips ready to greet his own, he saw instead that Igraine had retreated to a corner of the room, tightly gripping a cross and a rosary. When he approached, she screamed at him to stay away and invoked the protection of the Holy Virgin Mother to protect her from being shamed.

How can you be so cruel as to spurn my love? he asked her. But she pleaded with him not to come any closer, to be a decent Christian man and to respect her holy vows of matrimony. Feeling guilty and embarrassed, Uther left Igraine and returned to his own bed chamber. There he took a solitary light dinner and washed it down with enough bitter ale to guarantee his collapse into a dreamless stupor.

The King was woken by his seneschal, who told him the night sentries on the fortress ramparts had heard the gates burst open from the inside and saw several people stampeding away on horseback—knights, ladies, wagons piled high. After the sentries descended to the courtyard, the stable boy told them the horses that had gone belonged to Gorlois, Duke of Tintagel.

Uther then immediately ran to the rooms where the Duke had been staying, not even bothering to change out of his night clothes. But the rooms were empty. The Lady Igraine, whose tall swaying figure and tumbling blonde hair had brought him so much joy, was now gone from the castle.

The bustle and the noise had meanwhile roused several knights who had gathered in the Ling's chamber by the time he returned. They demanded that he severely punish the Duke. To flee his King and liege lord in the dead of night, without leave to depart, like a highway robber, was an insult too great to let pass.

But Uther did not want revenge. He felt ashamed, but also an aching emptiness without the Lady Igraine nearby. He needed her back for his peace of mind. He would not harm her, he swore, but rather he would gently persuade her of the sincerity and depth of his love. Once she understood how profoundly he felt what he felt, then she would not be so unkind as to deny her favors to him. All he needed was Merlin to tell him where she was heading, and he would dispatch his knights to bring her back.

Merlin shook his head and turned his eyes to the floor. After collecting his thoughts for a few moments, he answered Uther Pendragon: Your Grace, they are no doubt riding towards the Duke's lands and are likely nearly there. Your men will never overtake them before they reach one of the Duke's castles, where he can secure his wife behind gates, ramparts, and deep moats. You must write to the Duke and offer to make amends, otherwise there will be war.

Uther agreed the Duke was by now safely ensconced in one of his castles. It had been a long, tiring day. Everyone needed to rest, the King concluded.

Merlin took his leave and returned to bed. Sleep evaded him, though, as he worried what would happen to the kingdom of Logres. Igraine had clearly told her husband what Uther Pendragon had done. And the Duke no doubt felt affronted at the core of his honor. If the King did not make amends swiftly—if he did not give the Duke an honorable path to reconciliation—then something terrible might happen.

And something terrible did happen. Uther was dissuaded by his knights from offering conciliatory terms, as they insisted he was the wronged and insulted party. The King's seneschal issued a curt letter to the Duke demanding an apology and appropriate compensation for leaving the royal court without permission. The Duke wrote back that Uther was a filthy lecher who had sought to shame him and his pious wife. He renounced his previous vows of allegiance and loyalty to the crown of Logres and claimed to hold his lands and titles directly from God.

Once the Duke had openly declared himself a rebel, there was no choice but war. So Uther raised an army, marched on Tintagel, and laid siege to the Duke's castles. But the Duke's men stayed loyal to him, and his fortresses were well-stocked with provisions and carefully secured. The sieges dragged on inconclusively for months.

In the late summer, Merlin was summoned to the King's camp outside the stronghold where Duke Gorlois had entrenched himself. He was escorted to a private audience in Uther Pendragon's pavilion. After a rushed and distracted exchange of pleasantries, Uther fell down on his chair and burst into sobs. Once he had calmed down, he spoke to Merlin:

I cannot bear to live without being able to touch her. I had hoped to end this war quickly, but the Duke's defenses are too strong. Every day the manpower and the treasure of Logres dwindle because of this fighting amongst ourselves. I will prevail in the end, but the cost is too great—what will happen if my enemies abroad start raiding the coasts again? Will there be enough knights left in Logres to drive them out?

I have thought many times of offering terms, but I cannot bring myself to give her up—to promise that I will never lay my hands upon her. When I close my eyes, I see her face and her long golden hair, and I hear her voice, and my flesh trembles with longing. Help me, Merlin.

Looking at the King, Merlin was struck again at their physical resemblance: two short pudgy men with tangled beards, sitting in a camp of tall blonde knights mounted on warhorses. He felt a rush of pity come over him, although he could not tell if it was pity for himself or for Uther.

Merlin decided to help the King. He could make Uther appear in the guise of the Duke. As the Lady Igraine was being guarded in a different castle than her husband, Uther could travel to her, pretend to be her husband, and she would lie with him willingly, unable to tell the difference between him and her real husband. Uther Pendragon could sate his lust and learn there was nothing especially wondrous about this one particular woman.

Still, if the spell wore off too soon, Uther would be exposed and alone in his enemy's fortress, certain to be quickly captured or cut down. Merlin would need to accompany the King to make sure the enchantment held for a long enough time.

With these thoughts turning in his mind, Merlin answered Uther's plea for help: Your Grace, if you give me your word that this war will end if you lie with Igraine, then I will arrange for you to have your heart's desire.

You have my word, Merlin.

Your Grace, meet me at dusk at the edge of the camp with two strong horses. Tell no one what you are doing or where you are going.

And so at dusk, they secretly rode off. Once they had traveled far enough that the men in Uther's camp could no longer see them, Merlin led him into a thick forest where they dismounted and tied the horses to a tree. Then Merlin smeared both their faces with a particular crushed herb and rapidly recited a series of incantations.

Now, go over to the pond there, he told Uther, and tell me whose reflection you see. The King laughed when he looked down into the water: I am Duke Gorlois, he declared. And you are no longer Merlin—you appear to be one of Gorlois' knights.

They remounted their horses and rode confidently to the Lady Igraine's castle, arriving in the early evening. When the sentries saw their lord Duke Gorlois approach, they immediately opened the gates and welcomed him home. Uther thanked them and asked to be taken to his wife, for he said he missed her sorely. As soon as she saw him, Igraine threw her arms around the neck of the man who appeared in the likeness of her husband and smothered him with burning kisses.

That night Uther, in the guise of Gorlois, took his pleasure with Igraine, just as he had dreamed for so long. He posted Merlin, in the guise of a knight of Tintagel, as guard outside the bedroom door. Merlin could barely conceal his mirth. He imagined how ashamed Igraine would be if she knew she were ravenously embracing the short, ugly, brown-bearded Uther instead of her tall, strapping blonde husband. Despite all her pious Christian twaddle about the sanctity of the soul and the evils of the flesh, Igraine was proving herself to be a pathetic and easily humiliated slave to the very bodily things that her earnest Christian confessors railed against: Her eyes saw only flesh, not spirit, and they pulsated with lust at the sight—no, the illusion—of Gorlois' supple, muscular body. Igraine, he reflected, had not rebuffed Uther because of her sacred marriage vows to the Christian God, but rather because she was disgusted by the thought of touching a man whom she found physically ugly. She preferred a man whom she found physically beautiful, just like the birds and the beasts in the forests of Northumbria when it was their time to copulate.

When the sun rose, Uther and Merlin departed from the castle. Upon reaching the same secluded patch of forest, Merlin transformed them back to their right appearances. Uther was grinning madly with joy and swore he could not put into words the enormous gratitude he felt.

Matters turned out even better for the King when he returned to his camp. His seneschal rushed over to him, flushed with excitement, to tell the good news: After a rumor had circulated that Uther had fled his camp, Gorlois had been emboldened to charge forth from his castle and attack. In the ensuing battle the Duke had been speared through the chest with a lance, and then trampled to bits by his own confused and mammoth horse. The war was over.

Over the course of the next couple of weeks, Uther's barons and Gorlois' barons negotiated peace terms: There would be a complete amnesty for the rebels and no loss of lands, titles, or wealth, provided that the now widowed Igraine married the still bachelor Uther Pendragon. The Lady Igraine, having little choice in the matter, went along with the barons' terms and forced many smiles and appropriately conciliatory words from her mouth.

Shortly after the wedding, Merlin was summoned to a private audience with the King. Queen Igraine, Uther explained, was quite distraught. She had confided to him that after learning how and when her husband had died, she had realized that the man with whom she had lain that fateful night could not have been Duke Gorlois. She worried it could only have been a demon incubus who had ravished her through some kind of vile trickery.

But there was worse: Igraine was pregnant. She was sure it was the child of the incubus.

Uther told Merlin that he had decided it was best not to enlighten his new bride about what had actually happened on the night Gorlois died, but he did promise her that he would seek counsel with his court sorcerer, who would know how to deal with matters such as incubi and their spawn.

The King concluded: So what is your counsel, my Lord Merlin?

And then the two men burst into uproarious laughter. Merlin felt a malicious joy at the thought of the beautiful, graceful, tall blonde Queen being reduced to such silly hysterics.

When he had recovered his composure, Merlin offered to take the child right after the birth. The more he thought about this idea, the more he liked it: If the baby were a boy, then the child would be Uther's heir, and Merlin could teach him to be a just and wise King, better than Vortigern or Uther. Perhaps this whole tawdry adventure would result in the birth of a ruler for Logres who would bring peace, prosperity, and happiness to all the inhabitants of the kingdom.

And so it came to pass. Igraine, shrieking with superstitious terror, gave birth to a baby boy with a thick head of blonde hair, who wailed proudly as he entered this world. Merlin took the child, named him Arthur, and placed him in the care of foster parents whom he trusted.

As he grew up, Merlin would visit Arthur now and again, teaching him to act justly and to be kind and courteous. But he concealed the boy's true origins, both to keep him humble and to prevent future rival claimants to the crown from murdering young Arthur in his sleep.

When Arthur was seventeen years old, Uther Pendragon passed away from this world—but with no acknowledged heir to the kingdom of Logres. His five stepdaughters, the children of Gorlois and Igraine, had been married off to five foreign Kings to secure key alliances; each of these Kings now made noises about being the rightful successor to Uther. The barons of Logres protested that they would not swear fealty to a foreign ruler, but they could not agree amongst themselves who should be the new King.

With the threat of war looming, Merlin conjured a great boulder with a sword stuck into it to materialize in the courtyard of the largest church in Logres. He loudly proclaimed this wonder to be a sign from the Christian God that whoever could remove the sword from the stone was the rightful King. The archbishop and the common people readily agreed.

The foreign kings and the barons tried their luck, but none of them could lift the sword. Then came the turn of the knights and the squires, who similarly failed. In the end, only young Arthur, barely a squire, succeeded in removing the sword. The Church and the people hailed him as King by divine election. But the foreign Kings and the barons seethed, swearing they would never pledge their fealty to such a lowborn man. Merlin told them they were fools and said he would prove Arthur to be higher born than any of them.

He summoned a meeting of all the foreign Kings, barons, and bishops, as well as Arthur and the widow Queen Igraine. He directed the archbishop to present Igraine with the most sacred Christian relics in Logres, and she swore unwaveringly upon them that she would answer Merlin's questions truthfully. Then Merlin recounted to the entire assembly how he had contrived through sorcery and trickery for Uther Pendragon to share Igraine's bed, and how he had taken Uther and Igraine's baby to raise as he saw fit. He asked Queen Igraine to confirm the truth of his account—that she had fornicated with a man who resembled her husband but was not him, and that she had given up the child whom this stranger had sired upon her to Merlin's care.

The eyes of the gathered dignitaries turned now to the Queen. Her eyes, though, were looking at the floor, and her body trembled. She did not respond.

Answer me, upon your sacred oath, Merlin thundered at her.

Still looking down, she tried several times to speak, but kept breaking into sobs, which she then forcibly stifled.

There were many cries to stop this cruelty to a grieving widow—the heathen sorcerer, they said, was shaming a good Christian lady. But Merlin sneered back: You would not accept the judgment of the Christian God that Arthur is your rightful King, so you have forced the Queen to endure this humiliation to prove her son Arthur's legitimate claim to the crown.

Once more, Merlin demanded that Queen Igraine confirm that he had spoken the truth.

This time she managed to speak: Yes, it is the truth.

And with that, the Queen stood up and bolted from the room, never lifting her head up to confront the eyes of the nobles and bishops of Logres.

Arthur's royal bloodline was now settled, and Merlin's powers were held in even greater awe than before. Yet from that day onward, Merlin never received a pleasant greeting or a warm smile at court. He was respected, and frequently consulted, and none dared to threaten him—but that was all.

# VI. The True Importance of Magic

IT HAD BEEN months since Viviane had fled from Merlin. As was their wont, King Arthur's knights had scattered across Logres and the neighboring kingdoms, sometimes following royal commands to bring brigands (or worse) to justice and sometimes simply looking for a fight (which they insisted upon calling an adventure). The King himself had returned to his capital at Carduel. And Merlin was left to wander the countryside.

He strolled about the forests of Logres, and visited a lord here or there who had asked him to help with an illness in the family or a problem with the livestock. These were hard days for Merlin. Everyone he encountered felt distant from him, as if Merlin were submerged in a river and looking out at crowds frolicking on the dry land. No matter what he did, he found no joy, but only an itching, tiring restlessness.

Merlin understood his condition only too well: He was lovesick for the Lady Viviane. The memory of her image was the one thing that could, however briefly, lift his spirits. But then he would recall how she had run away from him, so full of hatred. He would remind himself yet one more time that it was hopeless to love her. She was young and beautiful and would no doubt marry a young and handsome nobleman—that is what the young and beautiful do, find each other, fall in love, marry, and sire another generation of young and beautiful people to repeat the cycle. He knew he was not beautiful; and if he ever forgot his loathsome appearance, the strained, poised politeness of the ladies of Arthur's court when they addressed him was reminder enough of the effort it took a highborn lady to tolerate a creature as hideous as he was.

Yet his soul stubbornly refused to stop longing for Viviane.

And then the vision started to come in his dreams, repeating each time he closed his eyes and drifted off to sleep: a hermitage in the forest, a square stone building with a crucifix over the threshold. Merlin would travel, in the body of a bird, to a tree branch overlooking this hermitage. The sun would be shining, and the other birds would sing their hellos and how-are-yous. Yet the happy scene would soon be interrupted. A huge man in black armor would walk up to the door of the hermitage, tear it off, and drag the hermit outside, howling and praying, to string him up on the tree right below where Merlin and the other birds were perched. The black knight would then turn around. A woman would scream—her face blurred, or blocked by something, although the voice was always familiar. With the scream, Merlin would be jolted awake.

Because this same dream came to him night after night, he grew convinced that some forest spirit or old god was sending him an omen, although he could not fathom what it was about. To solve the riddle, he penetrated deep into the Perilous Forest, wandering for several days until early one evening he found the square stone hermitage with the crucifix over the threshold, just as he had seen it in his dream. He knocked gently on the door. A ghastly thin, hairless man in a loose-fitting, coarse tunic answered—it was the hermit. He asked the hermit if he could spend the night and share a bite of bread and a cup of water. The hermit seemed not to hear him at first, but eventually invited him inside. Merlin was thankful that this particular Christian holy man seemed ignorant of his alleged demonic origins and satanic powers.

The hermit ignored his guest and retreated to his oratory in the back. He moaned his prayers in a rasping, terrified voice. Merlin helped himself to the stale bread and dusty water on the table near the door and soon fell asleep in a corner of the front room.

He woke to a loud banging at the door. In an instant, the door was knocked off its hinges and flew to the ground, letting in a rush of harsh bright sunlight. A huge man in black armor strode inside and went straight to the oratory in the back. Moments later, he dragged the hermit outside.

Merlin followed them out of the hermitage. There was a noose hanging from a branch of a large tree nearby. The black knight hoisted up the hermit and slipped his head through the noose's opening. The hermit did not resist, but mumbled his prayers quickly and faintly in Latin. Merlin felt unable to move or look away; he did not try to help the hermit. He was certain these events would soon reveal some hidden meaning.

Merlin suddenly heard a woman scream from another direction. He turned around and saw the Lady Viviane seated on a great black horse with her feet and hands tightly bound. The black knight was now heading towards her, still oblivious to Merlin's presence.

Merlin hurriedly spoke an enchantment, made several hand motions, and spit on the ground three times. Then he yelled: Sir Knight, your true love awaits.

At these words, the black knight turned away from Viviane and ran away madly chasing a deer into a thicket of trees, the clanking and clinking of his armor fading into the distance.

Merlin freed Viviane and helped her down from the horse.

What did you do? she asked. How much time until he returns?

Merlin laughed softly. My Lady Viviane, do not worry about that knight. I cast a love spell, quite potent, and from now, until the end of time, that deer will be the black knight's one true love. He shall have eyes for no one else, including you. You are safe.

He asked how she had become the knight's prisoner.

She answered: I was riding with my governess, the nun whom you had met, when the black knight came upon us. He killed her and tied me up, swearing he would do with my body what he wished. But first, he said, he had to finish riding to the man who had betrayed him, as his lust for vengeance was apparently greater than his lust for pleasure. He said the man he sought had been his closest friend until he abandoned him in battle, causing the black knight's stronghold to fall to a Saxon raiding party. The deserter claimed to have heard an angel's voice telling him to put aside the vain and bloody things of this world and to focus his soul instead upon contemplation of God's infinite and abounding glory. Heeding this command from Heaven, he became a hermit in the woods.

Viviane paused and looked down before speaking again: Thank you, my Lord Merlin, for coming to my aid. I know I have not always been kind to you, but many speak ill of you, you must know that, and I must be cautious. If it were suspected that I had lost my maidenhood … which the black knight, he had wanted …

The Lady Viviane sat down against a tree trunk, seemingly lost in her thoughts. Merlin was terrified that, if he spoke, he would say something that would chase her away again, so he kept a respectful silence and greedily took in through his eyes each part of her body. He had sorely missed the sight of her.

Finally, she spoke again: My Lord Merlin, please tell me, could I have used that same love spell to scramble the black knight's reason?

Certainly, my Lady, that spell or plenty of others. That is, if you were learned in the art.

But my Lord Merlin, aren't your powers unique, a gift from your demon father?

He shook his head. While I was gifted at birth, those gifts only made it easier for me to learn to be an adept. And I had the fairies as my teachers. Yet a mortal woman could learn much of the art—not everything, some visions would be denied to you—but much of it, spells and healing, could be performed by anyone who learns to command the spirits and the elements that surround us.

Will you teach me, my Lord Merlin?

# VII. A Happy Idyll

MERLIN HAD NEVER been so happy as he was in those following weeks with Viviane, living together amidst the ruins of the high Roman official's lush villa, deep in the woods and far from any village or farm. This house must once have been grand. It covered the entire hilltop, and if the forest were cleared—and perhaps once was—it would have commanded a sweeping view of the countryside. There were wide porticos of white marble, dimmed and smudged from decades of neglect, on which stood life-sized statues of men and women in earnest, forceful poses. Inside the villa were spacious rooms decorated with wall paintings of playful curly-haired men and women enjoying dinner parties on couches, or noble heroes fighting beasts and monsters, like a man with a bull's head, a giant with one eye, and a three-headed dog.

Upon first entering the ruined villa, Viviane had re-marked that the occasional scribblings on the walls looked like the Latin words the priests read from their books. Was this an abandoned monastery?

Far from it, Merlin answered. This was a villa built by an old Roman lord, a worshipper of the many gods of the groves and rivers of Italy, who had been sent to remote Britain by his Emperor. The homesick Roman had used his vast wealth to build himself a wondrous palace to remind him of Italy and its heroes and gods. He had even erected altars to those Italian gods of his. When he and the other Romans abandoned Britain, his gods made sure the trees grew thickly around the place to hide it from the Christians, who would have made it into a church or a monastery—who would have desecrated their altars. The old Roman gods still wait patiently for their worshippers to return, but they have no followers anymore.

You should give thanks to these lonely gods living in exile, far from their real homes by the Mediterranean Sea: They will keep us hidden from prying Christian eyes that would condemn you as a witch and burn you alive for consorting with a sorcerer and a demon's son.

And he smiled. Viviane moved her head slightly to the side and smiled back at him.

Each morning a raven, acting on Merlin's instructions, would caw in their ears to wake them. After breakfast, they would begin the slow, painful lessons. Merlin had never before tried to teach his arts to someone else, and he often had difficulty putting into words what he could understand intuitively. He could feel the rivulets of magic that skipped along on the wind's back, and he knew how to snatch whatever he needed. Yet explaining to Viviane how to listen closely to the air for the raw materials of a spell was difficult, to say the least. For the longest time, she simply could not hear the subtle whispers of the spirits and the elements swirling about her. He would grow tired and irritable and swear that teaching her was a stupid idea.

But the Lady Viviane would take hold of his arm, humbly apologize for being so dense, and beg him to continue. He would look up at her tall neck craning down to his short body and into her beseeching eyes. A shiver of both nervous terror and rapturous delight would rush up and down his skin, his heart would beat faster, and he would feel an overpowering urge to please this woman and win her gratitude. So he would try once more to teach her.

Over time her skills gradually increased. Her senses became attuned to the sparks of enchantment hidden about her. Merlin taught her which herbs heal and which herbs poison, as well as many spells and incantations, including the time of day at which they were most potent. All these things she learned, and as she learned she wrote them down in a little book.

Because these were the balmy summer months they slept outside, side by side on patches of soft moss just below the marble porticoes. She permitted him this favor, to lie next to her, so long as he did not touch her and remained fully clothed. He would fight off sleep as long as he could to listen to the gentle heaving of her breath. He would roll over on his side to face her, and try to smell her scent. Viviane always smelled to him like just ripened fruit. But soon enough she would roll over onto her other side, with her face pointing away from him, and he would fade into sleep with a melancholy, lonely feeling weighing down upon his heart.

After several weeks together in the old Roman ruins, Merlin worked up the courage one night to reach his hand over to hers and try to entwine their fingers. She snatched her hand back violently and bolted up, glaring down at him lying on the moss. She reminded him of the oath he had sworn: Before she had agreed to accompany him to such a secluded spot, she had made him swear, upon his loyalty to King Arthur and upon his parents' memory and the fairies and whatever gods or spirits he worshipped, that he would not attempt to molest her or take her maidenhood. Had he forgotten his oath? Would she have to flee from him again?

Merlin begged her to stay. He had not intended any harm—he was not going to shame her in any way—he had merely wanted to feel her soft, beautiful skin … to feel it … only a little.

Her body remained tense, and she looked at him with eyes pulsating with hate. Bewildered and scared he would lose her again, he burst into tears and again begged her to stay. He swore he loved her, loved her more than everything he had sworn an oath over, and he would never act to harm or humiliate her.

Then prove it to me by following your oath. A genuine lover will wait for his lady, for when she chooses to extend a favor to him.

But I fear that will never happen. Please, be kind—let me touch your fingers—just your fingers, and just briefly.

The Lady Viviane remained silent, but her features relaxed and her eyes softened. Even though he knew he had no good reason for this feeling, hope involuntary swelled in his breast and made his pulse race with anticipation for her reply.

She finally spoke again: My Lord Merlin, here is what I shall do for you. In return for proof of your devotion, I will hold your hands tightly and place one kiss on your check and another on the bald patch on top of your head. The proof I require is that you teach me three spells or the properties of three herbs, until I have mastered them. Once I have mastered those three pieces of your art, you will receive these favors from me. But for tonight, go to sleep and mind your oath.

So Merlin went to sleep a happy man, trembling with expectation for the morning.

Now he redoubled his efforts to teach Viviane. And she was as good as her word: At the promised intervals, she would approach Merlin, squeeze his hands tightly, and, with a smile, reach down to kiss his cheek and his bald spot. At the touch of her fingers and lips, he felt the world spin wildly and marvelously about, as if he was riding a huge red dragon soaring through the clouds.

But then the Lady Viviane would release her grip and step away. And even though she was no more than two or three feet away, his heart ached at the vast distance that had suddenly opened up between them. She was unreachable, untouchable, again.

# VIII. The Snake in the Garden

THE BLEEDING MAN explained to Merlin that Logres had fallen into chaos—Saxons had landed again, a huge raiding party, and King Arthur was fiercely fighting them off. This bleeding man, a handsome young knight, recounted how he had fought for his local baron against the invaders. Defeated in battle, he had fled deep into the woods, although not before Saxon arrows had pierced his flesh in three places and the point of a Saxon lance had lodged in his shoulder. He was weak from his wounds. Could the good people who lived in this forest help him?

Merlin laid the wounded knight down on a soft bed of moss close to the villa's portico and carefully removed the man's hauberk and mantle. He left him only briefly to find a particular herb nearby, which he then applied to clean the gashes and staunch the bleeding. The knight cried out in pain, but Merlin assured him this balm would help him heal.

A few minutes later, the Lady Viviane returned; she had been bathing. Merlin explained how the knight had found his way to them and asked her to fetch water and vegetables.

For the next few days, Merlin and Viviane tended to their patient together. He used the injured knight as a teaching aid, showing her how wounds bleed, where they tend towards rot and decay, and the proper way to apply different healing herbs. When they examined his body each morning and evening, he showed her how to tell if the lesions were healing or worsening, and what were the signs that the patient's food and drink were being digested properly.

In the beginning, the knight was asleep most of the time, and even when he was awake he would complain how the light hurt his eyes and made his head throb with pain. He sometimes screamed in terror and insisted he saw things that were not there such as Saxon knights charging at him or cackling demon imps in the tree branches taunting him about his sins.

But gradually the knight recovered both his strength and his reason. One afternoon, when Viviane addressed Merlin by his name, the knight called out: Are you the enchanter Merlin? Is that why you know so well how to tend to my wounds?

Yes, I am the enchanter Merlin. And you are fortunate that you found me, otherwise the rot that had begun to fester in your lacerations would have spread to your whole body, and you would certainly be long dead.

But why are you here, my Lord Merlin? King Arthur has sent messengers throughout Logres and Northumbria and Cornwall to find you, to summon you to his army. You must leave this place. I can tell you where the camp is. The lady—is she your daughter? She can look after me and help me gather my strength.

Merlin knew he should help Arthur, but to leave would be to abandon Viviane. And would she ever return to him? She ran away from him once, and she had threatened to do so again. She did not return his love, he knew that, but it gave him such joy to be near her and to receive her slight, grudging favors.

So he answered the knight: For the time being, I cannot join King Arthur's army. There are matters, hidden and secret and terrible, to which I must attend. When I am eventually able to do so, I shall answer the King's summons.

But the knight persisted—Logres needed Merlin now, crops and livestock were being burned and stolen now—he could surely attend to his other business later—how could he abandon his King, to whom he had pledged his fealty?

Merlin soon grew tired of arguing with his patient. He decided it would be easier for him, and a test of skill for her, if Viviane alone were to care for the knight.

This seemed a good solution at first. Viviane would take short breaks from her lessons to check on the knight's condition, after which she would seek Merlin's counsel about how to help him heal. He was impressed with how her skills were improving. She would return from the knight with her cheeks flush with joy, which Merlin took to be a sign of growing pride in her abilities as a healer.

But the intervals she spent with the knight became longer and longer. Left alone now for long stretches of time, Merlin absent-mindedly picked herbs and brooded. He could not understand why more time was required to tend to the knight as he grew healthier and thus less in need of frequent attention to his wounds.

Once he had picked enough herbs and vegetables to last for some time, Merlin spent his idle time exploring the ruins of the Roman villa. He tried to make himself marvel at the wealth and glory of the Romans, and to ponder deeply what calamity could have ever persuaded such powerful rulers to abandon the land they had conquered and retreat back to Italy. Yet no matter how hard he tried to force himself to think these edifying thoughts and to care deeply about the sweep of history and the passage of time, his mind kept circling back to the same few, obsessive thoughts, which would not leave him in peace: Where was Viviane, when would she return, how much he longed to see her.

One afternoon the wait proved so unbearable that he worried she had left him again. Merlin felt his heart weigh heavily in his chest and his palms sweat, his temples pound, and his stomach twist in knots. He tried to calm and focus his senses, to reassure himself she was nearby and there was no need to worry, but his efforts were in vain. He had to know where she was at that very moment, had to know— know, not guess—if she would return to him again.

From the opposite end of the large villa he walked toward the portico facing the bed of moss where the knight had been convalescing. As Merlin approached, he caught sight of the two of them through a broken doorway: Her head was on top of his, and her long red hair grazed the side of his body. Their arms and hands were entwined. He heard the hushed sounds of labored breathing. Feeling a sudden sharp pain in his ribcage, he retreated back to the farthest end of the ruined villa.

After sitting down upon a broken stone bench he looked at his feet and burst into tears. He should not be surprised, he told himself. She had never returned his love—she had never even pretended that she loved him back. Viviane was young and beautiful; it was inevitable that she would fall in love sooner or later—that is, fall in love with someone who was not him. And why wouldn't she prefer a handsome young knight to a short, fat old man who pathetically begged the favor of holding her hand?

He knew she would leave him. He would run out of magic to teach her. Or she would decide she had learned enough. Or she would grow bored with his special art. Or she would fall in love with a man as beautiful as she was. She would marry, yes, and have children, and sleep in a luxurious bed in a vaulting keep in the center of a vast fortress.

And then another thought came to his mind: He had taught Viviane vast and marvelous secrets, far beyond the knowledge of any Christian man or woman in Britain, and she had repaid him with only petty trifles—fleeting chaste kisses, quick touches of fingers. She had taken much from him, but given little back in return. She was in his debt, but as soon as the knight would be healed, she would ride away with him and never pay Merlin what was owed for the extraordinary wisdom he had revealed to her.

He decided he would take his proper payment and do it that night.

When darkness had fallen and Viviane had drifted off to sleep, Merlin roused himself and walked quietly to a secluded spot. There he mumbled a series of incantations and smeared three different varieties of herbs upon his face. He then went to a nearby pond to examine his reflection in the moonlight: He now appeared exactly in the image of the wounded knight, except restored to good health. No human eye could tell them apart; he was sure of it.

He went back towards the villa, to where Viviane lay sleeping on the moss bed. He knelt down and woke her gently. She opened her eyes and smiled at him. Her hands reached for his head, pulled him to her lips, and for the first time, Merlin felt the bliss of a passionate, tender kiss.

Then Viviane lifted his head back up to look into his eyes. She seemed on the verge of saying something loving, when suddenly her brow furrowed. Sitting up, she gripped his head violently and stared harder into his eyes. Merlin tried to break free, but having the knight's outward appearance did not give him the knight's physical strength.

She uttered a spell, and he quaked in terror. It was a seeing spell, and soon she would see him as he truly was. He finally broke loose from Viviane's grip. Fleeing back to the pond, he quickly undid the charm and returned to his normal shape.

Sleep evaded him that night. One moment he was certain that he must leave Viviane, that she would exact a terrible revenge for his betrayal of his oath to her. Yet the next moment he was just as certain that he should stay—after all, he had not shamed her or taken her maidenhood. He even tried to convince himself she would forget the matter, or chalk it up to a bad dream.

For the next couple of days, Viviane skipped her lessons with Merlin saying curtly that the injured knight was so close to a full recovery that she felt duty bound to devote all her time and energy to his care. When Merlin offered to help, so that she could rest a bit, she replied that she had been tending the knight's wounds for so long that only she could complete the task properly.

Merlin was left alone once more to wander about the spacious ruin and the surrounding forest, watching the sun gradually slither across the sky from dawn to dusk. He tried again to occupy his time collecting herbs and mixing potions, but once more he soon had picked and mixed all the herbs that were there in that place.

Still restless, Merlin studied the paintings on the surviving interior walls of the ruined villa. Although their colors had faded a bit, they were wonderfully vivid—the miraculous talents of those conquering Romans. They could do anything, win battles, build roads and bridges, and paint the most extraordinary pictures. He felt sad that such an extraordinary people had abandoned this country.

He found his way into what seemingly was once a back bedroom. On the wall was a painting of a muscular giant who had only one enormous eye set in the middle of his forehead. The one-eyed giant was kneeling down on the ground and reaching out with his hands; his face had a pitiable, begging expression. The begging seemed directed towards a woman running away from him, a beautiful olive-skinned woman in a flimsy white dress blown about by the wind. She was running towards a handsome young man wearing only a loincloth. He not only had two eyes set where two eyes should be, but those eyes were dark blue and his hair a mass of lovely tussled chestnut curls. The two beautiful youths smiled at each other warmly, so happy at their imminent embrace. They both ignored the desperately pleading one-eyed giant.

What should the giant do? Merlin wondered. He is in love, but with no hope for it. His deformed ugliness could never compete with his rival's fetching, soft, regular features. The giant should abandon these two—discreetly slink away—and leave them undisturbed to their passionate embrace.

Perhaps there was a one-eyed woman giant whom he could court. They could raise a family of one-eyed giants. Maybe even live in a kingdom of one-eyed giants where it was not only expected, but admirable and flattering to have only one eye in your head. Perhaps there the two-eyed would be shunned as monsters.

But it did not seem there was such a happy kingdom of the proudly one-eyed, because if there was, why would this one-eyed giant be so pathetically groveling for the favor of a conventionally pretty two-eyed woman? No, pleasant as the fancy was that the one-eyed could have a kingdom of their own in which they could be honored and adored, the one-eyed giant was the one who did not belong, the ugly wretch blighting the otherwise perfect sandy beach and blue sky and pair of young lovers.

So what to do then, Merlin's thoughts continued, if you love deeply but that love is not returned? The giant could try to live alone, but that life would be bitter, filled with hopeless craving for his beloved.

Or he could rid himself of his rival. A big strong giant like this one-eyed fellow could easily hurl a heavy boulder at those soft chestnut curls and supple, pretty limbs. He could use that boulder to grind the beautiful youth into a fine powder and scatter his bits into the sea. Then the maiden would have to turn to him—there would be no one else on that beach for her to love.

Merlin was startled out of his reverie by the sound of two voices laughing wildly—Viviane and her knight. The laughter kept going for several minutes, both his and hers, and it felt to him like sword thrusts stabbing into his chest. He hated Viviane because he knew she was about to leave him for that young knight, but he also could not bear to be apart from her. He felt love, and he felt hate, everything mixed up together, tangled and incoherent, raging in him like a fire burning an old forest to ash.

He started to sob, straining to cry out as loudly as he could because he wanted her to hear him. He wanted her to notice him again and to react—to direct her gaze upon him again. But it was no use. The lovers kept laughing, doubtless embracing each other, oblivious to the little fat man weeping in the far corner of the ruined villa.

Merlin eventually exhausted himself and drifted off to sleep. When he awoke, it was quiet. He walked to the portico, where he could see the moon shining brightly in the night sky. Viviane and her knight were fast asleep on the moss beds.

The sight of them, lying next to each other with such contented grins on their sleeping faces, filled him with a new wave of surging hate. He went back inside the villa, to where he kept his herbs and potions. After grabbing a handful of a particular variety of crushed flowers and a small flask of a greenish liquid, he walked back to the moss beds and approached the sleeping knight. With glee, he rubbed the flowers on the knight's chest and poured the greenish liquid on top of them. He rapidly whispered several incantations and then climbed up a nearby oak tree, from whose high branches he could see down below without being seen by others.

When the morning came and the sun had risen, Viviane screamed in horror. Her beloved's skin had turned green, his eyeballs had melted in their sockets, and his body had withered and pruned as if all the blood in him had been drained into a wine barrel. She called out to him, but there was no answer. She wailed and moaned, but no one comforted her in her sorrow.

Up in his tree, watching Viviane suffer so miserably, Merlin felt a pang of regret; perhaps this was too far, perhaps he had been too cruel. But no, she was going to abandon him, after all he had taught her and shown her. His only choice, he reminded himself, had been to hurl a great boulder to pulverize his rival.

# IX. The Wages of Sin

AFTER BURYING THE knight's body, Viviane said she wanted to leave the villa. His death was a sign the place was cursed—perhaps that was why the mighty Roman lord had abandoned it to the weeds so many decades ago. She was sad there had been no priest to administer last rites to the knight, but she was sure he was a pure soul who doubtless had little, if anything, to confess.

It was baffling, she continued, that the knight's condition had so suddenly and drastically worsened when he was on the cusp of fully recovering his strength. Could her teacher Merlin explain this marvel? Had he ever seen its like?

Merlin shook his head and mused about the unpredictability of fate and the limits of the powers of healers, even the most gifted and the most learned. Some mysteries, he said, were beyond his knowledge.

Viviane silently stared at Merlin for a long time. He tried to read her expression, but he could not make out what she was thinking—she was too perfectly still and calm. He felt increasingly uncomfortable under the heaviness of that stare—was she upset with him? Did she suspect him? Or was she comforted by his presence? Was she pondering whether to leave him?

Then Viviane at last spoke again: My Lord Merlin, you have taught me so many things, but I know almost nothing about you. Where did you grow up? Where did you live before you came to court?

So Merlin told her of his mother and his father and the fairies, and the forest with all its creatures, and the hill with a secret passageway to the fairy Otherworld.

Had any human ever entered the Otherworld? she asked.

Yes, once—a pair of lovers. The boy was the eldest son of a great baron. He was tall and handsome and a fearless knight. His father hoped for a marriage alliance with a family at least as equally wealthy and distinguished, if not even more so. But the young man had other desires. He would ride far away from his home into the outermost reaches of his father's lands, through woods and meadows, and in one such distant place he met a young woman tending her flock of sheep. She was so beautiful that the young knight immediately fell in love with her, and he courted her every day; he swore they would be married. When his father the baron found out, he sent his bailiffs to find this woman and cut her down.

Fortunately, the young knight had learned of his father's wicked plan ahead of time, and he raced out of the family's castle in the dark night to save his beloved. The two lovers rode deep into the forest. In those days there were not so many Christians yet in Northumbria, and the baron's son was loyal to the old gods. He beseeched them for help, and a fairy led the two lovers to the hill with the secret doorway to take shelter in the fairy Otherworld.

But happy as the lovers were in the otherworld, they could not stay there forever. The Otherworld is full of lilting songs and sweet fruits and colorful flowers, but if humans stay there, their lives will slip away quickly—time moves differently for fairies, and a few weeks of fairy time can waste away an entire human lifespan.

Still, the fairies took pity upon them, and hollowed out the interior of a crag at the edge of the wood to be the lovers' new home. Inside the cliff they constructed a luxurious, enchanted hall. There was a platter that was always piled high with food, no matter how much was taken from it, and a barrel that never emptied of wine, no matter how much was drunk. The fairies placed the two lovers there, where they lived out their days in peace and joy.

This place still exists. The door is both concealed and locked by enchantment, but I know how to find and open it.

Viviane did not respond at first, but stared at him again with the same inscrutable expression. But then her expression suddenly changed, as if the most wonderful idea had just occurred to her. She asked Merlin to take her to the lovers' hidden hall in the crag.

He immediately agreed, overjoyed that she was not going to leave him. They set off that day by foot to Northumbria. During the journey, the Lady Viviane went out of her way to be kind to Merlin, holding his hand as they walked, and stroking his beard as he fell asleep at night. She told him he would be quite handsome if he would only trim his beard and get the twigs out of it. That, and rub scented oil in his hair. Merlin felt himself blush, which, to his surprise, was not shameful but rather exhilarating.

She never spoke of her beloved knight, but rather filled Merlin's ears with praise—how wise he was, how many extraordinary deeds he had performed in the service of the Kings of Logres. She frequently expressed her deep gratitude for all that he had taught her, and she urged him to teach her even more, which he gladly did—so eager was he to please his love and keep her by his side.

When they reached the cliff where the lovers' secret hall lay concealed, Merlin spoke a charm in the archaic, singsong dialect of the old fairies. Then a white marble door appeared in the rock face. He spoke a second charm in the same language, and the door opened.

They went inside. The hall was brightly lit, although there were no candles or torches. The walls and the floor and the ceiling were all made from marble. Huge tapestries depicting unicorns at play in lush meadows hung on the walls of the vestibule hallway, which led to a dining room.

There, just as Merlin had said, was a platter filled with the rarest delicacies and a barrel from which they poured themselves goblets full of wine. When they had eaten and drunk their fill, Merlin urged her to keep walking further inside. The next room was a parlor, with couches and musical instruments, as well as a chessboard that would play against you as if the board itself were alive and was the other player.

After the parlor they came to another hallway sloping downward, which they followed deep into the bowels of the mountain. It ended at a door, which opened into a room with an immense bed piled high with red sheets, red blankets, and red pillows.

The Lady Viviane led Merlin to the bed. He marveled at the softness of the sheets, in which he felt like he was floating in the middle of a lake. She grabbed his head and kissed him passionately.

Then she asked him: Do you wish me to be happy? Not just happy in this moment, but happy always, happy forevermore?

Yes, very much so.

Would you do what I ask of you so that I can be so truly happy for all my days?

Of course, he said, of course, anything, I love you.

Viviane smiled sweetly and told him to close his eyes.

And he obeyed.

Now promise you will not interrupt me.

Once she had his word, she slowly and carefully spoke an incantation that plunged Merlin into a deep, paralyzing sleep. As she spoke the words of the spell, he had realized that he was about to be rendered helpless and unconscious, and for a fleeting moment he was seized with terror; but because he had been so happy those past few days, he could not bear to risk losing Viviane's favor—this was a bliss whose like he had never known. And they were in the lovers' special, secret palace, a place built specially by fairy magic for only kindness and passion. So he chose not to stop her sleeping enchantment when he had the chance. He wanted desperately to trust her, to feel safe with her.

It was a long time before he woke again, but when he did, Viviane was gone. He called out to her, but there was no response. He assumed she had returned to the dining room to eat again and thus she probably could not hear him calling from so far away.

He decided to join her. He was hungry, too. He got up, stretched and yawned, and walked to the door. But when he reached for the knob, it had somehow disappeared. He tried pushing the door, but it would not budge. Feeling confused, he attempted a series of spells, but none worked to open the door. He even tried spells that should have shattered the marble walls to tiny pieces, but they were also of no avail. Some new enchantment had been placed upon the door and room, too powerful for him to undo.

He waited for Viviane to return. Perhaps she could open the door from the other side. But she did not return. Merlin slowly recalled he had taught her spells that could have irrevocably sealed the door and the walls. Had he not been so lightheaded with love when he journeyed to this hall, he would never have revealed such dangerous secrets to her.

He sank down by the side of the bed and squeezed his face tightly together. Tears dribbled down his cheeks, uncomfortably sticky, but he did not bother to wipe them away. He reflected that this imprisonment was a fitting punishment for his great folly. Too late he now acknowledged once more the truth of what he was and what he would always be, and how he must sicken and disgust any beautiful maiden forced to look upon his ugly countenance.

With no means of escape, the great wizard Merlin died from thirst in three days. His body was never found and he received no proper burial. Even the fairies left his bones to rot in the bowels of the mountain.

# Other Books by Barak Bassman

Elegy of the Minotaur

Repentance: A Tale of Demons in Old Jewish Poland

King Solomon and Ashmedai: A Wisdom Tale

The Twilight of the Magical Siren: A Tale of Late Antiquity

The Leper Princess and The Court Jew

The Last Confession of Joseph della Reina

The Gifts of the Fairy Melusine

Necromancy of the Demon Maiden:
A Gothic Tale of Podolia